Amanda Coe is a script writer for film and television. This is her first collection of stories. She lives in London with her husband and young son.

GW00370730

A
Whore in
the Kitchen

AMANDA COE

A *Virago* Book

First published by Virago Press 2000

Copyright © Amanda Coe 2000

The moral right of the author has been asserted.

*All characters in this publication are fictitious and any
resemblance to real persons, living or dead, is purely coincidental.*

All rights reserved.
No part of this publication may be reproduced, stored in a retrieval
system, or transmitted, in any form or by any means, without the
prior permission in writing of the publisher, nor be otherwise
circulated in any form of binding or cover other than that in which
it is published and without a similar condition including this
condition being imposed on the subsequent purchaser.

A CIP catalogue record for this book
is available from the British Library.

ISBN 1 86049 813 2

Typeset in Perpetua by M Rules
Printed and bound in Great Britain by
Clays Ltd, St Ives plc

Virago
A Division of
Little, Brown and Company (UK)
Brettenham House
Lancaster Place
London WC2E 7EN

For Andrew

Contents

A Whore in the Kitchen

This is one of those sad, through the years kind of stories. Saddest of all is where it starts, 1972, and what I'm wearing. My mother really wanted a girl. What other excuse is there for making an eight-year-old boy wear two-tone slacks with chocolate brown top-stitching, beige to the knees, brown from knee to bottoms, where they billow amply over my invisible shoes? Plus my hair, practically back-combed, with careful curls tickling my neck. A pretty boy, and I resent it. I might have been perfectly happy being a girl, but I'm fully aware that I'm not. My mother grew to accept this, but until I was eight, there must have been some hope in her mind that I might switch. I had already discovered the difference of girls, thanks to Christina. I definitely didn't want to be one.

We moved the year of the chocolate-brown slacks. We were always moving, due to vagaries of my dad's business which I was too young to be interested by. This house was smaller than the last one, partly because of the mysterious business reasons, and partly because my older brother, Jonathan, had gone to university. We were the only Jewish family in the suburb, which was a new experience for us. Among other Jews, we were irreligious and unremarkable. In this neighbourhood, we felt fresh from the flight from Egypt. The teachers at my new school encouraged me to give presentations in assembly, and I sorely taxed my parents' meagre store of knowledge for material. My mother resorted to ringing my grandmother, to get the Hebrew right.

It was because of my denominational novelty that Christina asked to see my willy. She lived next door, with her mother. No father, no brothers or sisters – just the two of them. She was twelve. Although flattered by her request, I was also a little frightened.

'You don't have to show me if you don't want to,' she said, kindly. This disarmed me, and I obligingly pulled down my top-stitched flares. At eight, I didn't have the wit to ask to see anything of hers in return. Christina seemed unimpressed by my offering.

'Is it true you've had the end cut off?' she asked. I put her straight on that, but she didn't seem to believe me. 'It's very small,' she remarked, uncritically.

Strictly speaking, Christina wasn't my type. I already had a liking for blondes, and her hair was brown, chopped into an untidy pageboy. When I first met her she often wore bunches, tied with plastic bobbles. The orange or red or yellow spheres were imperfect because she took them out of her hair and gnawed at them as she spoke. When she had to go home, I enjoyed watching her re-tie her bunches, the deft way she took a clump of hair in one hand and wove the chewed bobble around it with the other, all without having to look. Girls had these arcane areas of competence, like the skipping they did with loops made out of elastic bands. French skipping, they called it, and boys were never allowed to join in. I didn't mind. I just liked watching.

Christina and I played together nearly every day of the summer we first moved into the area. My mother said she was a tomboy, because our games sent me home dirty, but there was no tree-climbing or ball-kicking involved. We preferred enactments of plots distilled from favourite books and TV programmes into one rambling epic. There was a lot of finding treasure, and being captured. Christina usually inveigled me into tying her up with a skipping rope, so that she could escape from her bonds and come to rescue me. This wasn't difficult, as I was terrible at knots (my mother claimed the Scout organisation was anti-Semitic), and she often released herself before I had found a suitable site for my own incarceration.

Our other favourite was a game called 'bang bang, you're dead'. This simply required one player to shoot an imaginary gun at the other, saying the words 'bang bang, you're dead'. The other player then had to die in the most spectacular fashion possible, staggering, groaning, falling to the ground, twitching, reviving and finally expiring. Marks were awarded, grudgingly, out of ten. It was this game that covered me in mud and grass stains, to my mother's despair.

'Why can't you play nicely?' she lamented, scrubbing at the knees of trousers, but I didn't take a blind bit of notice. Christina was an exacting judge, and I was determined to beat my personal best of eight and a half, won when I winded myself by executing a straight pratfall on to a concrete pavement.

I never bettered it, as it happened. Once the school term started, Christina and I immediately saw less of each other. Christina was already at senior school, and I had new friends to make at the local junior. It hadn't occurred to me that it was unusual for a twelve-year-old girl to spend most of her time with an eight-year-old boy, even a pretty one.

It is 1977. I am thirteen, recently bar-mitzvahed. I have yet to have my growth spurt, although things are definitely happening, biologically speaking. I spend much of my time in my room, headphones clamped over my ears. My mother has abandoned her campaign of feminisation. I am no longer pretty.

Christina and her mum still lived next door. Christina was seventeen. She had left school the previous year and was learning how to be a secretary. She had become very tall and thin and what my father embarrassingly called a 'dollybird'. (Her mother he called a 'glamour puss'.) It would have been perfectly reasonable for Christina to be dismissive of me, but she always stopped for a chat whenever our paths crossed. Sometimes we waited at the same bus stop together in the morning. Christina, her brown hair artificially flicked back off her face as though strict sections of it had been exposed to tormenting winds, smoked Benson and Hedges and told me how much she hated secretarial college.

'It's so fucking boring,' she declared. 'I am so *fucking* bored.'

I was flattered by her attention. I hoped that casual onlookers might mistake us for boyfriend and girlfriend, although the disparity in our heights made this unlikely. And of course Christina had a boyfriend, a real one. His name was Brian Stone and he was in the sixth form at our school. He was shorter than Christina but even I could see that he exuded sadistic charm. He had narrowed his tie and his school trousers, as only the coolest did, to match his narrow eyes. Although Brian was the sort of sixth-former who singled me out for casual victimisation if I happened to get in his way, my association with Christina meant that he acknowledged me on school property, bestowing a meagre kudos I sorely needed.

'He's thick as shit, Brian,' Christina told me, not without pride. We were on the top deck of the bus together, both travelling into town. 'Mind you,' she exhaled a ribbon of smoke, 'he's thick where it counts as well.' She grinned. I was careful to look unshocked.

'He's like you,' she added.

Brian was Jewish? This was news to me.

'A roundhead.'

I pretended to know what she meant. Eventually, I worked it out for myself. They broke up quite quickly, although Brian continued his debt of courtesy to me until he left the sixth form. I grew used to seeing Christina with plenty of other boys, and I soon could identify the type she went for, the type who would last for longer than five minutes. She liked boys who were trouble, or looked it. Wiry boys, with legs as thin as arms, torn T-shirts and drainpipe jeans. Pale boys, with shadows under their eyes or spots on their chins. Boys whose hair was the most eloquent thing about them, dyed red, shaved into a Mohican, tumbling down their backs. Boys who weren't always boys, but sometimes men. These men had the same look, but desiccated – freeze-dried boys. I thought of them all as vampires. They shared a nocturnal quality.

1977 turns into 1978. I've grown. I spend even more time in my room. I'm very much in love with Christina, but simultaneously with Helen (the sister of my friend Nigel Perrin), a girl who works in the baker's, whose name badge says Jenny, and Debbie Harry. I've started to smoke, furtively. When you're fourteen, most of your preoccupations are furtive. At night I smoke out of my bedroom window, accessorising my melancholy. Sometimes I see Christina coming home, snogging one of her swains against the front door, then shutting them out. Once, almost unbearably, I caught a glimpse of her blind white breast as a boy called Phillip pulled at her top. Phillip didn't last long, but I've worn the image threadbare for my own purposes.

'Hey, peeping Tom,' she called out one night. Her illuminated face poked out of the fanlight above next door's bathroom window. I jumped violently, and dropped my cigarette. Although our houses prided themselves on their detached state, they almost touched on the near side. My bedroom faced Christina's bathroom. She was kneeling on the sink unit, her body obscured by the frosted glass below the fanlight.

'Get a good look, then?' she asked. Her tone was friendly.

'I was smoking,' I protested.

'Give us one, then,' she demanded. Not entrusting the packet to the drop, I proffered a single cigarette. We managed to make the handover with both of us at full stretch.

'You're too young to smoke,' Christina told me, and lit up. She didn't mean it. 'What d'you think of him, then?' she asked.

'Couldn't tell,' I told her. 'I wasn't looking, anyway.' It was true that I hadn't made out the latest vampire's features, what with the dark, and the way his head had dipped in shadows to devour Christina's mouth.

She smoked, tapping the ash down into the abyss between the houses.

'What's his name?' I asked her.

'Pete,' she said. She pulled her fingers through the underside of her hair, which was recently and rather unsuccessfully permed. 'He's married,' she added, self-importantly, 'but you can't break up a happy marriage. That's what they say, isn't it?'

No one I knew said this, but I didn't get out much.

'Anyway,' she said, 'I'm just having a laugh. We haven't even done it yet.'

The light from the bathroom haloed the unnaturally frizzy outline of her head. I admired her habitation of a world where doing it was an inevitability, and just a matter of when. A world where you might even consider doing it later, rather than sooner. She chucked the cigarette end into the garden and retreated. I watched her moving shape behind the frosted glass. I listened to her brushing her teeth, then having a pee. The toilet flushed, and I was alone.

Christina searched out the tiny beacon of my cigarette most nights after that to share the progress of her affair with Pete. She had left secretarial college and was working as an assistant in an electrical goods store. Pete was the manager there. He was twenty-eight, ten years older than her.

'I think this is it, David,' she confided in me. She had had her hair streaked, which made her look older, and her eyebrows were plucked almost out of existence. Her eyes trapped liquid points of light as she leaned forward to offer me a cigarette. I took it, my hand shaking slightly.

'It's what?'

I knew that she had started sleeping with Pete, although the euphemism was inappropriate. Since he was married, they couldn't actually spend any nights together, but relied instead on quickies in his car or in the shop after closing. Christina told me that Pete had asked her not to wear knickers to work, just to turn him on. She found it arousing herself, she said. Sometimes they pretended that he was an intruder in the shop, and he overpowered her. In that way. Apparently that was good fun too.

'Love,' she said. 'I think I'm in love with him.'

I couldn't think of anything to say to this, so we smoked in silence for a while.

'He's different.'

'What's different about him?'

She discarded her cigarette and wrapped her arms around herself, shivering a bit, smiling.

'You wouldn't understand.'

I didn't see Christina for a few nights after that, although the whole family could hear her and her mum shouting at each other next door. The night that she next appeared at the window, she looked pretty terrible. Her mascara had smeared round her eyes and her hair needed washing.

'I'm moving in with Pete,' she told me. 'We've got a bedsit.'

'What about his wife?' I asked, dumbly.

Christina shrugged, twisting a strand of hair. 'What about her? You know what they say – you can't break up a happy marriage.'

'That's what they say,' I said.

1984. I am in my second year at university, where I'm ostensibly studying history. I wear second-hand clothes, dead men's suits. The only time I see my parents is when I go home for vacations, reluctantly. I am going out with a modern languages student called Julia, who is neurotic about food and sexually intense.

I took Julia home to meet my parents, largely at their insistence. To my chagrin, they got on extremely well. She attributed this to their Jewishness, which she saw as a sort of cultural trademark guaranteeing natural warmth. Naturally we were put in separate rooms, but managed nights of corridor creeping, at Julia's instigation. I had never been the subject of erotic obsession before, and was beginning to find it difficult to live up to.

Christina's mother had moved some years ago, and there was a proper family living next door in her place. My mother didn't know what had happened to Christina. I thought of her as I smoked out of my bedroom window. My smoking was still officially unacknowledged within the house, and I didn't have the courage to come out about it. The new tenants had put up a mobile against the bathroom window for their small children, and it was the shapes of this that I saw as I inhaled and exhaled into the night; a parade of ghostly ducks. From the bed, Julia demanded to know what I was thinking about, hopeful that it would have some application to her. I made something up.

The day before we were both due to go back to university we were in a pub, having an argument about a packet of salt and vinegar crisps. Julia hadn't wanted me to buy them for myself because she would be tempted to eat them. She had eaten three, and was upset. I was telling her that she was crazy.

'David?' I looked up and there she was. Christina. Her hair was punkily cropped and peroxided, and it was this difference I noticed before I realised she was pregnant. She looked pretty. I embraced her for the first time, and for the first time I was taller than she was. We laughed at this. I introduced her and Julia, although I could see they weren't going to hit it off. Christina was with a group of friends, but agreed to stay for a drink.

'Just orange juice,' she admonished me, with a gesture to her belly. She still cadged a cigarette, although she made a point of stubbing it out halfway through and ostentatiously waved the smoke away from her, disowning it. I asked if the baby was Pete's. She was amused by the assumption.

'He couldn't make a cup of fucking tea, let alone a baby. Anyway, he went back to his wife, didn't he?'

'So . . .' I gestured delicately towards her pregnancy.

'Don't be rude,' Julia objected, but Christina reassured me that she didn't mind. The father was a furniture-maker called Kev, and they lived together in Wales. Christina was just back for a few days visiting her mum, who'd been ill. She made a tippling gesture against her mouth to denote the nature of her mother's illness. This was news to me.

'Oh yeah, all the time,' said Christina airily. 'Pissed as a fart. Why d'you think I liked coming over to your house when I was a kid? No wonder I never had any friends.' She put down her empty glass, then smiled at me ruefully. 'Those trousers.'

'What trousers?' Julia asked, alert and protective.

'Thanks a lot,' I said to Christina. 'So it's all – and everything with this bloke?'

'Oh yeah. The real thing, definitely. You know what they say.'

'He's not married, is he?'

'No,' she said, nonplussed. 'What they say, the key to a happy relationship, right –', she included Julia in this confidence – 'is to be a whore in the kitchen, a maid in the bedroom – no, hang on . . .'

Julia was laughing. Christina smiled, ready to laugh at herself, but uncertain. 'That's not right, is it?'

'A whore in the bedroom?' I suggested.

'Trust you,' said Julia, proprietorially.

'That's it,' continued Christina, more confidently. 'A whore in the bedroom, a maid in the living room, and a cook in the kitchen. That's what you've got to do.'

'D'you get to be a mechanic in the garage?' Julia asked,

with pedantic jollity. Christina laughed politely. Before she got up to join her friends, we scribbled down our respective addresses. Christina said that she and Kev were thinking of moving back from Wales after she'd had the baby, to be closer to her mum. She kissed the top of my head as she went.

'A whore in the kitchen,' Julia giggled, disparaging, and reached for her fourth crisp. Beneath the table, I removed her hand from my crotch.

1991. A bad time for me. I am working as a solicitor, which both exhausts and understimulates me. I am too tired to think of looking for another job. I wear suits off the peg. My hairline looks as though it is receding, although this could just be paranoia. I have been living in London with my girlfriend, Bryony, who works in publishing, but things are not going well between us and we have decided that I should move out, since it is her flat. I try to see my parents every weekend, because my father has recently been diagnosed with prostate cancer.

When my father was admitted to hospital for the operation on his prostate, I went home for a week. My mother had been knocked sideways by Dad's illness, and had even abandoned her lifelong dedication to housework. With me there, she at least had someone to cook for. The sadness in the house was unalleviated by my presence. Instead, I added to it my sadness about Bryony, and the other sadnesses of my life. We were heavy with it. The days, punctuated by hospital visits and meals, were as long as days in adolescence. It was a relief to go to bed, earlier than normal so that I could lose another infinite hour.

I knew that Christina had moved back, and lived not far away with Kev and their son Dominic. We had kept in touch just enough to have current addresses. At the end of the week, unable to face another evening with Mum and the telly, I rang Christina up and suggested we go for a drink. She explained that I would have to go to her house, since Kev was away working and she couldn't get a babysitter for Dominic at such short notice. She didn't sound any different.

I was anticipating something small, a council house, but they lived in a snug Victorian terrace, spacious inside and filled with furniture that Kev had made. Dominic answered the door with Christina. He was in Scooby Doo pyjamas, and he didn't look like her at all. He hid behind his mother when I tried to offer him some sweets that I had brought.

'It's all right, Dom,' said Christina equably. 'He isn't a perv. You're allowed to take them.'

His arm shot out from behind her and grabbed the bag.

'What do you say?'

An unforthcoming silence.

'He's missing his dad,' Christina explained. She told Dominic that he could have two of the sweets and then he would have to brush his teeth and go to bed. He took his time as she held the bag out for him, agonising, then selected what seemed to him the biggest in the perfectly uniform bag. He put one sweet in his mouth and ran upstairs. Halfway up, he emitted a tremulous thank you.

Christina gave me a look and took me through to the kitchen. She was as thin as she had always been, and she had grown out her hair, brown again, so that it fell past her shoulders. I couldn't remember her hair like that since we were kids. She looked a little tired.

'The posh stuff,' she exclaimed, examining the label on the bottle of wine I had brought, fishing for the corkscrew. She offered me a cigarette from a near-empty pack on the table. Still Bensons. I declined.

'Don't say you've given up.' She poured the wine.

'Go on, then.' I took one. I had given up, largely. Bryony didn't like it. There was a cry of 'Mummy' from upstairs. Christina excused herself and went to put Dominic to bed. While she did this I looked at photographs which were fixed to the fridge with magnets shaped like hamburgers and ice-cream sundaes. From the photos I established that Dominic inherited his red hair from his father. Kev, sparely built and with a confrontational smile, was recognisably a vampire.

'Where is Kev?' I asked, when Christina returned to the kitchen. She explained that his furniture-making had dried up, and he had taken on building work to make ends meet. He was away in Chelmsford on a job. She laughed when I asked if she was working.

'Me? No. You know what they say. Why keep a dog and bark yourself?'

She poured me more wine. We worked our way through the bottle, and the packet of cigarettes. Christina had more of both, and, with a glance upstairs, also produced some grass. She told me about her mother, and about her and Kev. They had nearly split up for good when Dominic was five and the furniture-making had started to go under, but had managed to patch things up. I told her about my dad's illness, and about Bryony. I lifted my hair up at the front so she could see the lengthening of my forehead.

'You're imagining it,' she told me. We lapsed into reminiscence, largely about her previous boyfriends. According to Christina, I made things sound better than they had been.

'If Dom was a girl I'd worry about him,' she said. 'You know, being like I was.'

'There was nothing wrong with you,' I said, handing back the spliff.

'You don't know.' She sat facing me with her feet up on the couch, her thin toes, denatured by tights, close to my thighs. 'I'd see the girls at school, going around together, you know, best mates. It was like I gave off the wrong smell or something. Maybe it was with Mum, or being the only one. I never knew the right thing to wear, or whatever. When boys started paying me attention – it was like my birthday had come.'

Without forming the impulse, I touched her feet. It was like tripping a spring that propelled us together. Even just kissing, I was apprehensive that Dominic would come downstairs and see us. Christina reassured me that he always slept through. We grappled on the couch, not waiting to remove all our clothes. I was probably clumsy, but she smiled at me afterwards. She poked my bare stomach with her foot.

'That's new,' she observed. Her foot descended, playfully. She grinned, remembering.

'Unfair,' I said.

She made some coffee, and after we had drunk it I left. It would have worried my mother too much, spending a night alone. Christina didn't mind. She hugged me goodbye with unsentimental affection.

'It'll be funny when we're old,' she said, as I pulled on my coat. 'Can't you see it? You and me in the old people's home, cadging fags.'

'Deal,' I said.

Beneath the wine and the grass, I was unfogged by sadness for the first time in weeks.

And now. I stopped being a solicitor some time ago. I run my own consultancy from home, making a lot of money for not much of my time. None of my friends understand how this can be, and I scarcely grasp it myself. My hairline is definitely receding. I'm in love. She's called Jane. Plain Jane, she says, although she's far from it. We're getting married in the summer, nothing fancy.

We've bought a house together. Jane, who is very organised, but not dogmatic about it, helped me clear out my stuff before I moved. She pulled her hair into a ponytail before she started, weaving the elastic around the bunch of hair without looking. She meant business.

'What's this lot?' she asked, kicking a cardboard box with disintegrating corners.

'It's part of the archive,' I told her. This covered old phone bills, letters, university essays, tax returns and the like. The boxes had been kept in the cellar and reeked of damp. Another woman might have suggested that I throw out the whole cascading mess. Jane bought expanding files so that the archive could be housed less malodorously. To oblige, I spent some hours decanting the many pieces of mouldy paper into the fanned cardboard compartments.

Naturally I read everything as I put it in its place, slowing down the process. There was a Christmas card from Christina, dated four years ago.

'Maybe we'll meet up in the New Year,' it said. We hadn't. 'Love from Christina and Dominic.'

Right then, I waded across the banks of papers and went to the phone. It was a Sunday afternoon. Christina answered on the fourth ring. She sounded a little distracted.

'I've got Ellen and Dee Dee round,' she said, as though we'd spoken last week. I had no idea who Ellen and Dee Dee were. 'I'm cooking.' This was hard to imagine. I asked her how she was. Fine, she said. Did I know that she and Kev were no longer together? I didn't.

'We're better off without him,' she said. 'How's your dad?'

I told her that he'd died nearly a year ago, and she said that she was sorry. We let the next few sentences absorb that sadness.

'You with anyone new, then?' I asked, eventually.

'Nah. I'm off men,' she told me. In the background, Ellen or Dee Dee laughed disbelievingly. 'I am,' she said offstage, then to me: 'I'm waiting for you and me and the old people's home.'

'Can't wait,' I said.

'What about you?' she asked.

'I'm getting married,' I told her. There was the smallest pause, then she laughed and said how great it was. I talked a bit about Jane, and how we'd met.

'I'm really happy for you,' she said, and it sounded meant. The voices in the background were getting louder.

'Look, can we have a proper talk another time?' Christina asked.

'Let's. I just thought I'd tell you – oh and I'm moving.'

She got a pen and wrote down my new number, repeating it back to me. 'Call me when you're settled,' she said. I said I would. We put the phone down.

By the time Jane arrived, all the papers were tidied away. We loaded the files neatly into her car. She shut the boot on them and kissed me. Then we drove off, intent on our new house. When we got there, the files went into the garage, behind boxes of Jane's childhood Puffin paperbacks. They're always there if we want them. But as she pointed out, it'll probably be years before either of us opens those things again.

Assassin

No single incident catalysed Laura's attitude to Fay Knatchbull into a definite dislike. Since Fay had started teaching that autumn, her aggressive queries about departmental procedure, her appropriation of books that left another class short, a tendency to bring up irrelevant points in staff meetings — none of these endeared her, but they couldn't be considered professionally incriminating. Trivial encounters were more corrosive — the way she stood slightly too close when speaking to you, her lack of compunction in taking the last spoonful of staffroom coffee, along with an accompanying reluctance to make a drink for anyone else when she was boiling the kettle. And she was an irritant to the eye, Laura decided, with her fondness for outsized prints in livid pinks and fuchsias and purples, which gave a cadaverous sheen to her complexion and underscored the rabbity rims of her lower lids. It was when she homed in on this feature, as Fay took the last chocolate biscuit during a departmental meeting, that Laura realised the facets of her distaste had crystallised into something unexpectedly substantial.

Fay spat biscuit crumbs as she proposed an alternative to the school's traditional summer term production of Shakespeare.

'I know it's heresy to say it but it's not relevant to them, is it? Surely they'd rather do something with a bit of life, a musical. We did a fantastic *Guys and Dolls* at my last school. Or what about devising something from one of the texts they're studying?'

Isobel Matthews, who had directed the plays for the last eleven years, grew carelessly rigid. Jim Lake cleared his throat, fruity with nicotine.

'You won't have had the pleasure of seeing one of Miss Matthews's productions, but liveliness is something they're certainly not lacking in.'

'In which they're not lacking, surely,' murmured Frank Burrows, for his own benefit.

'Oh, no offence to you, Isobel,' said Fay, 'I'm sure you've done a fantastic job all these years. I suppose I'm just offering new blood sort of thing.'

Jim Lake raised his eyebrows to Laura, ironising dark apostrophes. Laura didn't reciprocate. As head of the English department, she was contractually obliged to transcend personalities. And besides, she was reluctant to feed Jim's bloated self-esteem, gorged as it was with the daily adoration of teenage girls and staff members.

'Well maybe you could offer your services to Isobel on *Midsummer Night's Dream*,' she suggested to Fay, then stood, orchestrating a flurry of paper-shuffling which closed the meeting. Isobel made a rictus of response as Fay bore down on her. Laura heard Frank Burrows intone 'Lord what fools these mortals be' as he drifted out of the room.

Martin was loitering in the kitchen, his coat on, when Laura got home. He did this, hovering near the door, insisting that he was on his way out as he nattered on, usually when Katie was trying to do her homework. Laura and Martin had been married for seventeen years. Martin had left her, in that he no longer lived in the marital home, and she did. But it had been a consensual abandonment, which had taken place almost too gradually. When he had first got his flat Martin still came home for dinner most nights, and spent entire weekends with her and Katie. At this stage a brief flare of frantic sex surprised them both. It soon died down. Martin's possessions ebbed out of the house, until no material pretext remained for his visits. Finally Katie suggested to her parents that their separation be put on a more formal footing. They turned this into a family joke – splitting up for the sake of the children – but obliged. Only now had they started to have rows. Laura was amazed by her new capacity for provocation by Martin, whose views had become so familiar that their marital conversations had taken on the tenor of imaginary dialogues, often leaving her unsure if the two of them had spoken at all. Now everything about him incensed her, from his political views to his dress sense.

'I'm just going,' he said, waving a book at her. 'Milton,' he explained. She snatched it from him.

'That's mine.' She showed him her name, inscribed in megalomaniac undergraduate script.

'I know, hope you don't mind, I couldn't find the Norton edition for love nor money.'

Martin was also an English teacher. His departure from the school in the early stages of their separation had resulted in the vacancy now filled by Fay Knatchbull. Laura tried and failed to find an objection to his borrowing her book.

'I want it back, mind,' she said peevishly. From behind a cairn of biology texts, Katie sighed.

Martin went. Laura poured herself some wine, and Katie sighed again. Laura told her to stop it. They ate their serially microwaved dinner in the space on the table between the books, then cleared the plates and remained, Katie to finish her homework and Laura to do her marking.

Laura wondered sporadically if the unvarying quality of her days signalled depression. She didn't feel actively miserable in the way that she had in the last two years with Martin, but she was aware of a life lived in the pages of magazines that eluded her. Other women, apparently, had friends and took lovers, updated their wardrobes each season with key items, investigated cosmetics, planned holidays, agonised over their careers. They designed their gardens and revamped their living rooms. All of these verbs were alien to her. She didn't even read novels any more.

'We should go out some time,' Fay Knatchbull said to her, one day in the staffroom. 'For a drink, I mean. Spinsters unite. Well, not spinsters, you know what I mean. On the pull.'

Laura vibrated the back of her throat equivocally and busied herself putting milk in her coffee. She knew that Fay was divorced or separated. Fay's earrings, wooden parrots, dangled at the periphery of her vision.

'What's happening with the play?' Laura asked, inclining her head to give the appearance of eye contact.

'It's brilliant,' said Fay, and reached over for the milk carton. 'I've press-ganged some of my Year Nine boys to be fairies, would you believe. I think Isobel's a bit worried, but I mean, you know that incredible energy they've got at that age. If we can just harness it.'

'Straitjackets,' suggested Jim. He ground his butt end, smoked to the very line of the filter, into an ashtray.

'Have you seen what the little fuckers are up to?' he asked.

'What?' said Laura.

'They've refined tag into this game, they call it Assassin.' He picked up the kettle, just emptied by Fay, and crossed to the sink to fill it. 'I think we can applaud the evil genius of Jay Bellamy, it bears the hallmarks.'

'Assassin?' Fay skipped out of Jim's way.

'They all have a "hit". Say Jay has to get Mandy and Mandy's after Aziz.'

'Isn't she always.'

'They can only get each other in the corridors or the canteen or the hall – classrooms are off limits. So, Jay gets Mandy, Mandy's dead, so he's now after Aziz, who's after someone else, and on it goes until there are only two left. Hence, assassin.'

'I hope guns are involved,' grunted Frank Burrows. There

was the sound of resonating metal as he tossed a sheaf of unmarked Year Eight homework into the staffroom bin.

Rounding a corner on her way to the next lesson, Laura sidestepped the hurtling figure of a plump little girl, being chased by a boy much smaller than her. Laura raised her voice and they froze in their tracks. Assassin, she assumed. She could hear them resume their chase the moment she was out of sight.

Laura's Lower Sixth set were studying 'The Wife of Bath's Tale' for A level. Any lesson after lunch was always a struggle, but in summer term marshalling concentration was almost impossible. Also, the set's ability varied to such a degree that she was always spinning plates with them, distracting Anthony the Oxbridge certainty with an etymological teaser while dashing back to reassure Lindsay, who transcribed everything she said with round-handed incomprehension, that she could definitely underline marriage as a theme.

'So, do you like the Wife of Bath?' Laura started, purposely bland. Seventeen pairs of eyes sluggishly second-guessed her – was the correct answer yes or no? Breaking against their silence, she could hear unsettled waves of noise from the neighbouring class. Laura chose a face.

'Nicky?'

Nicola Richards, cynosure of male attention, twined out one butterscotch curl and stared down into her cleavage for inspiration.

'Erm, dunno, yeah, I like her I suppose. I like that she doesn't care what she looks like, like she wears these like really stupid clothes and has a gap between her teeth and everything.'

Anthony the Oxbridge certainty writhed over his desk, handsome and fanatical. 'But that's precisely the point, surely – she's proud of her garters but Chaucer makes us see that they're ridiculous. He's laughing at her. Anyway, all that external stuff's from the prologue.'

Nicola blushed, rebuked and confused. Laura wished Anthony could moderate his zeal.

'So do you think Chaucer likes her?' Laura asked, guiding them into deeper water. The pattern of background noise underlying their talk suddenly resolved itself into a sharp female shout, verging on a scream. It was the voice of an adult, coming from the adjoining classroom. The kids looked at her to license their response. Laura decided to ignore it. She repeated her question. The shout exploded again, too loudly this time to be ignored. Laura excused herself and went out into the corridor. Now she could identify the voice as Fay Knatchbull's, careening out of control.

'Sit down!' she was shouting, almost shrieking. 'That's it, I've just about had enough of the lot of you. Either sit down or you're all in detention. I mean it.' There was an exaggerated, acoustic clatter of desk lids and scraping chairs. 'I said sit down now!' Fay wailed. Laura firmly opened the door. It took a couple of seconds to register that Fay's Year Seven group were supposed to be moving their desks into a participation-friendly 'U' shape. Some wielded the desks like four-legged shields, catching each other in the backs of the knees and provoking instant retaliation. Others were punting their neighbours' bags across the room, while a few played frisbee with their pencil cases. Anarchic exhilaration carried their twelve-year-old voices to the edge of hysteria. Fay stood helpless in the middle of the tumult. When she saw Laura it was with the relief of a besieged homesteader welcoming the cavalry.

'Mrs Bryant,' she pleaded. Laura hung on to the edge of the door.

'I'd appreciate you keeping the noise down, Mrs Knatchbull,' she said crisply. Before Laura swung the door shut she caught a vivid moment of Fay's face, its astonished recognition of abandonment. Laura returned to her class, resisting the curiosity in their attention, and the afternoon limped on. The noise from Fay's classroom scarcely abated.

In the car park after school, Laura saw Fay skirting its margins rather than take a directly diagonal route and encounter her again. In spite of herself, she called out.

'Would you like a lift?'

Fay started and looked behind her. Then she did a grateful splay-legged trot to Laura's car, hurrying as if she thought Laura might think better of the offer and speed away without her.

Laura tossed the heap of books occupying the passenger seat into the back of the car. Fay got in and hitched into the worn upholstery.

'I only live round the corner,' she said anxiously.

'That's OK,' Laura said crossly. She felt furious at her own compulsion to generosity.

'I'm sorry about 7J, little monsters. The weather doesn't help,' Fay continued. 'They just want to be outside all the time. Who can blame them, I'd rather be playing rounders as well. I mean how many times can you read *Lord of the Flies?*'

'You'd be surprised,' said Laura, chilly.

Fay's mauve skirt spread over the gearstick. Laura started the engine. They reversed past Jim Lake, pinned against his Astra by a brace of little girls wearing alarming amounts of eyeliner.

'Another two bite the dust,' remarked Fay. 'What's the story with Jim? I mean, how married is he?'

'He and Carol have a good marriage,' Laura said, pompously and untruthfully.

'He's a mega-flirt though, isn't he? Not that I blame him, I enjoy a good flirt as much as the next woman.'

Laura turned up the news on the radio, hoping to baffle further attempts at conversation. 'He can't help the way he looks,' she said.

'Oh I see.' Fay's tone was saturated with meaning. Laura wished she could kick her out into the moving traffic. 'It's like that, is it?' Laura checked the rearview mirror and ostentatiously failed to reply. 'With you two I mean,' Fay persisted.

'No,' Laura said. She avoided meeting what she was sure would be a complicitous smile.

The traffic flow out of the town centre was moribund. Fay turned down the volume on the radio and then, in her own unmoderated tones, told Laura the story of her marriage. She related how she and her husband had married two weeks after meeting on holiday in Crete. He was much older than her, and had been married before. The sex, she said, was mindblowing. Fay was convinced that she had met her soulmate, but within a couple of months she had faced up to the fact that her husband was an alcoholic. He only drank at nights, so it didn't affect his work as a contractor, but he was sinking a bottle of whisky at a time. Still, she was convinced that she could make it work. Then just before their first anniversary she came home to find he'd cleared out. He'd gone back to his first wife and he didn't want any further contact with Fay. He'd destroyed every photograph in the house, including their wedding photographs. Laura was at a loss how to respond to this.

'Not great for the old self-esteem,' said Fay, doggedly pumping buoyancy into her tone as though inflating a recalcitrant lilo. 'But you know, onwards and upwards. It's first right then stop almost immediately.'

Laura swung the car round the deserted road of the new estate. Fay's house was a neat, shrunken ersatz-Georgian box. She suggested Laura come in for coffee, but Laura said that she had to get home for Katie.

'I thought you said Katie was fifteen,' Fay challenged her, suddenly verging on the aggressive. This took Laura aback.

'She doesn't like being in the house on her own. And I said I'd drive her to a friend's.' Laura felt the superfluity of her second lie.

'Some other time then. *Mille grazie.*' Fay slammed the car door and ran, slightly pigeon-toed, up to her miniature porch. Laura drove away at speed. But she felt burdened by Fay's confidence, as though doomed to give house room to a gift that in no way accorded with her taste.

It was in the final week of term that Laura came upon Isobel Matthews weeping in the corridor outside the school hall. Her twiggy arms were propped on one of the sunken window bays, supporting her thin, heaving body.

'Problem?' asked Laura. It was not unknown for Isobel to get emotional at this time of year, when a production was imminent. Isobel snorted back a supply of tears. She fixed on her usual smile.

'Oh you know, creative differences. I swear, Laura, this is the last time I do the bloody thing.'

Laura reminded her that she said this every year.

'I mean it this time. Bloody Fay can bloody well take over.'

'What d'you mean creative differences?'

Isobel looked at her frankly. 'What do you think?'

This was the time, Laura knew, for her to withdraw into dispassionate mediation, but Isobel's distress enticed her to the brink.

'Surely it isn't that bad,' she said, exploratory rather than reassuring.

Isobel composed herself with a juddering sigh. 'It's more that bad than you can imagine.'

'I can imagine,' said Laura. Her sympathy was freighted with the full weight of her own dislike. Isobel flashed her a smile of pure relief.

'I could have a word with her,' Laura offered. Her own eagerness surprised her.

Isobel wrapped her arms across her chicken-bone chest, shivering. 'Oh I don't know, what could you say? It's not anything she does, really—'

Laura saw Isobel's face change colour.

'Isobel?' It was Fay. Too late to warn them, the hall's

swing door marked the end of its arc by hitting the wall. 'I
need you to have a look at the rude mechanicals – I think I
was right but see what you think.'

It was impossible to tell if she had heard them or not,
given the habitual discordance of her manner.

'If you've got a minute, Fay, I'd like a word,' said Laura.
Fay shrank back, as though in the presence of a despotic
and unpredictable parent. It struck Laura, with considerable
irritation, as a purely synthetic performance.

The staffroom was empty. Laura gestured Fay into one of
the laxly sprung armchairs and took the adjoining seat. Fay
angled her chair so that they were sitting knee to knee.
Despite her posture of submission, she looked Laura in the
eye with a defiance Laura recognised from attempts at rep-
rimanding fifteen-year-old girls. For the first time she
wondered what Fay thought of her.

'Is it about Tim Young smoking?' Fay asked. Tim Young
was the fifth-former playing Bottom.

'Smoking?' echoed Laura.

'Isobel seems to think there'll be some almighty outcry if
he's allowed to smoke on stage. It's a good bit of business
with a roll-up. I mean he smokes anyway, for God's sake.'

'Oh. No, but I don't think we should be encouraging
him. And the Head's very anti-smoking. He'll probably shut
you down if he sees anyone lighting up.'

Fay rolled her eyes.

'It's, there's also, just more generally, Fay – Isobel's quite
a sensitive soul—'

'I noticed.'

'Well . . .'

'Have I been putting my size sevens into it?'

'I think you have to remember that she's directed the plays for years now, and she's used to doing things a certain way. I'm just saying, you could, well maybe you should take a bit of a back seat, tread carefully.'

Fay's normally bloodless skin flushed to clash with her blouse. Her gaze was locked on her lap, where one thumb harried the shredded cuticle of the other.

'OK, point taken.' Her voice sounded thick. Laura was alarmed by the possibility of her crying.

'Sorry,' she said. 'You know what it's like. We're all inclined to get set in our ways.'

'All I've done is tried to help.'

'I know, and it's appreciated, really—'

The door crashed open and Jim Lake rushed in, alarmingly drained of persona. Fay stood, so suddenly that her chair tipped on to its back.

'Thank God,' Jim addressed Laura. 'I've got to ring an ambulance. Richard Veng's broken his leg.'

'Football?' she asked.

'No, the stupid little fucker's jumped out of a window.'

Fay offered to ring the boy's parents while Laura accompanied Jim to the playground. There, they dispersed the ring of titillated cronies gawping at the unlikely angle of Richard Veng's right leg. Although over six feet tall, Richard was only fourteen, and he gripped Laura's hand unselfconsciously as she reassured him that help was on its way. Garrulous with shock, Richard told them how he had been trying to evade Jay Bellamy, who was pursuing him in Assassin. Jay had run him to ground in one of the science labs since lessons had finished over an hour before, and knowing he had to get home, Richard had taken the desperate measure of jumping out of the window rather than give himself up. Laura waited for Jim's sarcasm, but he just took off his jacket and wadded it into a cushion for the boy's head as Richard gabbled on in detail about all the other 'hits' he'd made in the game.

'I've rung your mum, Richard.' It was Fay, striding towards them. Richard's grasp of Laura's hand grew tighter.

'I'm going to get done,' he groaned. Fay surveyed the scene.

'You shouldn't try to move him,' she announced. 'I used to do St John Ambulance.'

'We haven't.' Laura flicked her eyes away from Jim's quick glance, aware of Fay's avid surveillance.

'Certainly looks like a break,' Fay said. 'Quite a nasty one too. No more football for you, Richard.'

Richard started to cry. 'It really hurts,' he wailed.

Only one of them was needed to accompany Richard to the hospital with the emergency crew, but the current of communal urgency bore both Laura and Jim into the ambulance when it arrived. Fay trotted after them, but the attendant curtly informed her that there was no more room.

'I am his form teacher,' she appealed to Laura, but Laura engrossed herself in ensuring Richard was comfortable on the stretcher. The doors slammed and they drove off. Through the porthole windows, Fay receded, vainly waving Jim's forgotten jacket.

'Ambulance chaser,' grinned Jim. 'What were you doing

when I came in, anyway? She looked like she was about to hit you.'

Laura saw Richard was taking everything in with adrenalin-fuelled acuity. He still held her hand, which was cramped and sweaty from his grasp. '*Pas devant*,' she said to Jim repressively.

'You can be quite frightening when you want to be,' Jim told her.

Mrs Veng was already in the neuralgically lit waiting area when they arrived at the hospital. Like her son, she was a six-footer. Laura was glad to benefit from the woman's assumption that Jim was in charge, since, despite Jim's vagueness about the 'horseplay' that had inspired Richard to jump out of the window, she was furious. They gratefully left her to accompany Richard into X-ray.

'Christ,' said Jim. 'You'd think Jay Bellamy was a pushover compared to her.'

Reluctant to surrender to anticlimax, they agreed to wait until they knew the results of Richard's X-rays. Jim announced that he was dying for a fag and Laura went outside with him.

'So what's going on with Fay?' he asked, lighting up.

'Nothing,' said Laura. 'You know, just a word in her ear.'

Jim dragged on his cigarette. 'I could think of a few.'

'Thanks.' Laura's mouth felt taut with professionalism. Jim flicked ash.

'I've wanted to say, about you and Martin – I know it's always difficult. Sorry, anyway.'

'Thanks.' She was surprised.

'You seem to be coping.'

'Whatever that means.'

Jim delicately drew the end of his cigarette against the wall, twirling it so that all the dead ash fell away, exposing a tiny core of live orange.

'Any time, you know, if you want to talk or anything.'

Laura nodded and thanked him again. She hadn't wanted to talk until he suggested it, but his expression belied the invitation he had just issued.

They shared a taxi back to the school. Laura couldn't remember the last time her life had necessitated a taxi ride. Their two cars were isolated in the car park, empty spaces apart, like pieces on an abandoned chessboard. Jim's jacket was on the bonnet of his car, precisely folded, presumably by Fay. He shrugged into the jacket and waved goodnight to Laura, his grin a vice around his cigarette. Laura watched him get into his car and start it. The prospect of her own company, she realised, was utterly unpleasant. She didn't want to go home, but it was her only route. Jim drove away. Laura lifted her hands, as though about to play a piano chord, and gazed at them. She registered that she still wore her wedding ring. At the edge of her vision, something fluttered. Beyond her hands she saw there was a piece of paper flapping on her windscreen, pinned by the wiper. She removed it. Fay's writing veered below and above the printed lines of the exercise paper, roundly looped. The ink was turquoise. The note asked Laura to call her with news of Richard, but by the time Laura got home and told her hospital saga to Katie, she'd almost forgotten the request.

Richard Veng returned to school, heroic in a cast that stretched from thigh to toe. Jay Bellamy was upbraided, and Assassin was publicly banned by the Head. As longed for as a childhood birthday, the last day of term arrived. By morning break, some of the staff were making their first visits to the serried wine boxes supposedly off bounds in the staffroom until lunch. Frank Burrows, who was retiring, didn't even attempt to attend his lessons. He appropriated a wine box for his sole use and sat in his favourite chair, nursing the box on his lap like a pet.

At lunchtime, the school drained of pupils and the general drinking began. The elation of release burned off after the first couple of hours, and once the Head had made his speech and departed, the dedication to oblivion became less expansive. Cliques formed around the remaining drink reserves, smokers allocated their dwindling cigarette supplies only to cronies, and there were attempts to establish departmental hegemony over the ghetto blaster.

Laura hadn't been so drunk since Christmas, and not so pleasantly drunk since well before then. She inhabited a vast smile and spoke very little. Frank Burrows had become seized of the conviction that everyone at the party was trying to rob him of his wine box, and he spat florid but repetitive abuse at anyone who approached.

'You whoreson cur, you eater of broken meats, you cream-faced loon – a pox, a pox!' he shrilled at Jim, who patted him companionably on the shoulder as he passed. Jim raised his glass at Laura. She mirrored the gesture, beaming.

'All right?' he shouted, over the punishing backbeat imposed by the musical tastes of a junior geography teacher. Laura nodded.

'Surprisingly, yes.'

'What?'

Laura shook her head. 'Yes.'

Jim earnestly waved her over to the door. She followed him obediently out into the corridor.

'I couldn't hear you,' he shouted.

'I can't remember what you said,' Laura told him.

'Never mind what I said, what about you?'

'I'm fine,' she smiled.

'How's Martin?' asked Jim.

'He's fine.'

'I'm pissed,' Jim informed her.

'Me too.'

They continued down the corridor, shedding revellers. Jim opened the door to an empty classroom and waved Laura in with pantomime chivalry. After he'd closed the door he shook out an empty cigarette packet.

'Oh dear,' said Laura. He reached inside his jacket and took out a virgin pack.

'No problem.' He offered her the pack, tokenly, and lit up.

'Seriously, how is Martin?' asked Jim.

'Fine.'

'He's a bloody good bloke. I know I haven't said it or anything but I'm really sorry about you two, you know.'

Laura lolled against a desk. 'You said, thanks.' A cliché floated by. 'It's all for the best, really.'

Jim lurched forward and they kissed, messily. His mouth was like a meaty ashtray. Laura pulled a strand of her hair out of the way of his mouth, then clamped his backside, less yielding to the touch than it looked. They staggered against the desks and finally broke apart. Laura looked at the door, which didn't lock from the inside. Jim stroked her breast.

'I don't think, here . . .' Laura said. Jim raised his eyebrows, daring her to it.

'Where, then?'

'Later,' she said, then primly, 'We're supposed to be going to the play. *Midsummer Night's Dream*.'

'I'm pissed,' Jim groaned, then, brightening, 'No one'll know, if they're all at the play——'

Laura protested that Isobel would notice their absence. Jim pointed out that she would be backstage.

'Go on,' he wheedled. Laura capitulated. They agreed to meet back in the classroom as the curtain went up.

Laura led the way back to the staffroom. She stopped off in the toilets, strategically, and splashed cold water on her face. She felt it a moment after it had hit her skin. Laura reminded her distant reflection of her status. She drank from the tap, ineffectually, and applied lipstick. While she was doing this, Isobel came in, the tendons in her neck strung tight with nervous tension.

'You haven't seen Fay, have you?' she gasped. 'I need her to help with the make-up.'

Fay's absence at the party struck Laura with retrospective clarity. No wonder she had felt so untethered, without Fay standing reproachfully at the margins of conversations, or puncturing repartee by demanding explanations of in-jokes, or doing her Ancient Mariner routine about her marriage. Ancient Mariner and albatross rolled into one. According to

Isobel, Fay hadn't been seen since she'd finished lessons that morning. Laura was blithe about this, until Isobel pointed out that the entire department was supposed to be going on to Fay's after the play to continue Frank's send-off. What if they turned up to an empty house? Laura suggested phoning her. No one had her number, and the office was locked, Isobel informed her triumphantly. Isobel's appetite for a crisis had clearly been whetted. She even suggested ringing the police.

The dull gravity of responsibility reasserted itself. 'OK,' Laura said, 'I'll go round there and find her myself.'

She was just sober enough to recognise that driving would be foolish, so she walked. When she reached Fay's street, Laura hesitated among the identical houses, unable to call the number to mind. A likely house had a 17 on the door. She rang the bell. After a few seconds, the door was opened by an ingenuous-faced young man with a sleeping baby clamped to his shoulder. Laura apologised, and told him that she was looking for Fay Knatchbull. They both whispered, to avoid waking the baby. He pointed her to number 21.

Prolonged ringing of Fay's doorbell brought no response. Laura crouched down to call through the letterbox, hanging on to the door handle for support. There was still no answer. She moved to the front window, which gave her a view of the living room and part of the kitchen through its laminated diamond strips. The walls were an inoffensive pink, and there was a sofa in a deeper shade. It occurred to Laura that the colours suited the furniture much more than they suited Fay. The sofa, chairs and a side table were pushed against the margins of the room, exposing the fitted carpet, its pile freshly furrowed by the vacuum cleaner. Balloons clustered from the doorway and at a mirror. Although Laura couldn't hear anything through the double glazing, the stereo fascia's leaping display of blue lights indicated that music was playing within.

Laura moved round the house to peer into the kitchen window. Cling-filmed platters of sandwiches and lilliputian pizzas crowded the work surfaces. Clearly Fay was expecting them all. Laura tried the door handle, and stumbled as it opened into the kitchen.

Once she was inside the house, Laura didn't call out again. It felt like the *Marie Celeste*. The air, permeated by soft soul pulsing from the living-room stereo, was heavy with polish and air freshener. Seeing the plates of food, Laura felt hungry. She lifted a corner of cling film from a plate on top of the microwave and pulled out a small triangular sandwich.

In the living room, a lilac balloon which had come adrift from its mooring at the mirror rested incongruously on the pristine carpet. It chased ahead of Laura when she entered, like a living thing trying to escape. Laura trapped it against the wall with her foot, delicately. Then she brought her other foot down on the balloon, squeezing it to the limits of its internal pressure. It didn't burst. She applied the other foot, jumped a little, but it just absorbed her movement. Pins, she remembered, produced the most satisfying noise, jabbed into the taut surface. She found a cake skewer in one of the kitchen drawers and returned to the living room. The pop was farcical, a cartoon sound effect.

Still holding the skewer, Laura abandoned the pennant of forlorn rubber and stood on the coffee table to reach the cluster of balloons above the mirror. As she strained to reach the first, sausage-shaped balloon, her hip caught a pot on the mantelpiece. It landed intact, insulated by the carpet, but its contents scattered across a large area. Laura jumped down. Odds and sods were flung across the room — a book of matches, rubber bands, misshapen paperclips, some buttons, two grimy mint imperials. She picked up a broken wax crayon, blue-green. The wallpaper invited her. Perhaps this would be better, after all.

She started on a patch of paper near the window, hidden by the swags of the curtain. The crayon skated slickly over the paper, darkening the floral pattern into uniformity. It was surprisingly strenuous, maintaining the pressure necessary to obtain an even effect, and it quickly wore the crayon down. Laura stopped scribbling. Above the dark patch she had just created, she sketched the profile of a face in feathery, broken strokes. Only when she took the crayon from the paper did she realise it was Fay's face, in extreme and infantile caricature, the nose and mouth almost meeting, witchily. It was pretty good. She finished it with stringy hair and parrot earrings.

The crayon was now an unworkable nub. Laura allowed the curtain to fall back over the wall, hiding her work, and turned to look for the felt tip that had rolled out of the pot next to the sofa. A whimper of shock automatically leaped from her mouth. Fay stood at the door, a towel turbaned around her head. She was wearing a blouse with an elaborate neckline and below, only mushroom-coloured tights over knickers. She gripped a hairbrush as if it was a cudgel. Her face was momentarily vivid with terror then, seeing Laura, her expression broke into a delighted smile of welcome. Laura felt herself smiling back, forever.

'You nearly gave me a heart attack. I thought you were a crazed axe-wielding murderer or something,' said Fay.

'I came to see if you were all right,' Laura told her. 'No one had seen you, we were worried.'

'Thought I'd topped myself?'

Laura picked up the spilled pot, apologising.

'I wanted the party to go with a bang,' Fay said. 'Get everything sorted. You've caught me *sur le hop*, I'm afraid.'

'Well, as long as you're OK,' said Laura. 'I'd better get back. The play . . .'

'Oh don't go back to the boring old play, stay and have a drink.'

Fay skittered to the kitchen. The greasy scrap of wax crayon was warm against Laura's palm. She had no pockets.

'We can have a chat before the others arrive. You've never told me much about yourself.'

Fay brought out a plate of sandwiches along with the two glasses of wine. Her uncompleted outfit, with the marmoreal tights, made her look like she had been arrested in the middle of some mythical transformation.

'Right. This is the life. Cheers.'

They tapped their glasses together.

'D'you know,' said Fay, tucking her legs beneath her in the armchair, 'this is the first time anyone's been in the house since I moved here? Except me, I mean.'

Laura thought of Jim, the empty classroom. She slid the crayon deep into the cleft between the cushion and the sofa arm. Then, with the other hand, she raised her glass to her mouth and swallowed the warm, bitter wine.

'Cheers,' she said.

Help

The shop had been in business for nearly fifteen years. Along the same street, boutiques had come and gone and chain stores had stayed, but Quelque Chose occupied a niche apart from either. It wasn't exactly a clothes shop, although clothes were part of its stock. Outside, beneath the name, *precious objects for special occasions* was inscribed in careful gilt italics. Cleo, the owner and manager, didn't like to hear it described as a gift shop. Gift shop, in Cleo's opinion, suggested tacky cards and pot-pourri. She didn't stock pot-pourri, and the cards they sold were all selected by her to be tasteful.

'If I start selling pot-pourri, shoot me,' Cleo said to Vanessa, her number two. 'Those candles are the thin end of the wedge.'

Recently they had bought in ecclesiastical candles from Greece, with a dolorous Madonna printed on the paper wrapper. They were selling briskly, but Cleo knew that for her own self-respect, she couldn't always give the public what they wanted. For fifteen years she had preserved an effortful balance between her own taste and the need to keep the shop from receivership. In low patches, usually when she was marking down stock she loved just to shift it, she said,

'Sod it, Van. I'll start selling the tat they want – serve them right. We'll stuff the place with disgusting dolls and plaited things and novelty fucking teapots.'

This mood always passed unacted on, as Vanessa knew it would. Vanessa was used to riding out Cleo's low patches. She had been working in the shop since Cleo first opened it, on the proceeds from a tenaciously fought divorce. The fact that this had been from Vanessa's brother-in-law in no way precluded her from accepting Cleo's offer of a job. Vanessa's own husband, Liam, was deep into an affair with her best friend and her children were both at school. She needed diversion. One of the great things about working for Cleo, at least at first, was the impossibility of inhabiting your own emotional climate in her presence. She was a turbulent generator of mood, and for Vanessa, soused in despondency, there was a bracing quality to Cleo's gusts of outrage and storms of manic goodwill. And she had only ever worked part-time.

Lately, this had become a bone of contention. Public taste had entered a phase which coincided with Cleo's eye for stark shapes and unlikely colours and for the first time ever, the shop was flourishing. Aided by a rave in a glossy magazine (although it was rude about the name), afternoons spent eking out coffees and chatting to the odd faithful customer evaporated into memory. Cleo had to increase the frequency of her buying expeditions, which had previously been twice a year, to as much as once a fortnight. This meant leaving Vanessa in the shop on her own, fastidiously wrapping purchases and writing out invoices by hand, as an impatient queue formed on the other side of the counter. Vanessa had never worked mornings, or Thursdays and Saturdays at all. Now she agreed to cover the occasional morning, and a Thursday or Saturday where necessary. But she refused to make a more hardened commitment.

'You're a stubborn little cow,' Cleo bellowed, almost resigned. She extended a hand, weighted with rings. 'Please, Van. What else have you got to do?'

'Plenty,' said Vanessa, more calmly than she felt. 'You know I've got the house to sort out.' Liam had finally moved in with Vanessa's former best friend, leaving her with their large converted farmhouse but only half their furniture.

'Oh sod the house!' Cleo howled. 'It's a shit-hole anyway, that place. I don't know why you don't sell up and move into town, instead of rattling around on your own out there.'

Since Vanessa wasn't persuaded, Cleo was forced to advertise for a part-time assistant. No one she interviewed seemed in any way suitable, until a customer, seeing the card Cleo was removing from the window, mentioned that her daughter was looking for a job. She was re-taking some A levels, and a part-time position would suit her. With little hope, Cleo told the customer to send the girl along for a chat. She turned up as she and Vanessa were closing after a hectic Friday. She introduced herself as Lizzie, although her mother had referred to her as Elizabeth. She had a fresh, highly coloured face which made one think of costume dramas.

'This is such a cool shop,' she declared, looking around with ingenuous excitement. Cleo and Vanessa both took to her at once. For a start, her enthusiasm seemed genuine. And her vigorous, energetic prettiness and open manner suggested that she wouldn't sulk if asked to make coffee or dust shelves. Cleo offered her the job immediately.

'Really?' Lizzie asked, thrilled.

'I always trust my instincts,' said Cleo, enjoying her largesse. 'You have to, darling, in this business.'

Lizzie started the following day, Saturday, their busiest. On Monday, Cleo reported to Vanessa that it looked as though she would work out. She had had a little trouble in mastering the till to begin with, but had picked it up by the end of the day. And she was chatty to the customers.

'Nice to get away from the menopausal gloom as well,' laughed Cleo. Vanessa couldn't help feeling a little hurt. Seeing this, Cleo added, 'Oh stop being so fucking sensitive. Me, darling, not you.'

A week later, when Cleo had to visit a ceramics importer in London, Lizzie and Vanessa worked together for the first time. It was a Friday, and Vanessa came in to relieve Lizzie over lunch. The girl was meeting a friend, but still returned promptly within the hour.

'You could have taken a bit longer,' Vanessa told her. 'It's never busy around two.'

'Oh, that's really nice of you,' said Lizzie, smiling warmly as she took off her cardigan. 'I didn't want you to think I was trying it on.'

As Cleo had approvingly mentioned, Lizzie was full of questions. She wanted to know about the stock, what sold and what didn't, where it came from, what happened if a customer wanted to return anything. And what was so remarkable, and so pleasing, was that she genuinely wanted to hear Vanessa's opinions on these matters. What did she like best in the shop? What least? Who were the worst customers, from her point of view? Did she have things from Quelque Chose in her own home? Where did the ring she was wearing come from? In conversation with Cleo, Vanessa was used to being an echo chamber rather than a participant. But by the end of the day, with no end to the onslaught, she had relaxed into being quite talkative. It was novel to be the subject of so much attention.

Vanessa went home after closing feeling agitated, as though she had drunk too much coffee. Thinking about the day as she drifted off to sleep, she panicked a little, wondering exactly what she had said to Lizzie. She then rebuked herself for paranoia. She and Cleo had become just too set in their ways. And she liked Lizzie a lot. It was impossible not to. She was a nice, genuine girl.

'Lovely, isn't she?' said Cleo proprietorially, when Vanessa broached her opinion the following Monday. 'A real find.' Concentrating on the window display, she positioned a lacquered paperweight in desirable relation to its neighbour. She knelt back to appraise it, then swivelled her gaze, underlined with kohl, to Vanessa.

'You've made quite a hit yourself,' she remarked, in mocking tones.

'Really?' asked Vanessa, flattered. 'What does that mean?'

Cleo moved the paperweights a fraction closer together. 'Lizzie thinks you're very elegant,' she said, her tone glancingly disparaging. 'She seems quite taken with you. She kept going on about what a brilliant figure you have.'

'That's nice of her,' Vanessa said mildly, smothering her surprise.

It was true that Vanessa was bird-like. She always had been, whereas Cleo was more than big-boned. But of the two, Cleo was notoriously the more stylish.

'You've always had a good figure,' Cleo said dismissively, standing up. 'It's just a shame the way all this Liam business has aged you.'

In instalments over the next weeks, interrupted by demands for stock in different colours or more appropriate sizes, Vanessa confided to Lizzie the story of Liam's iniquities. Or rather, Lizzie extracted it. In fact, the process of intensive questioning which Lizzie used to do this helped to cast the breakdown of Vanessa's marriage in a palliative new light. Vanessa's version of events had been that Liam had, with some justification and predictability, grown tired of her and had an affair, and this account was more or less corroborated by Cleo's outbursts about the fate of all women over forty, unless they were blessed with good genes or resorted to plastic surgery, or were her. But Lizzie didn't see it in this way at all.

'But you were married when you were practically my age, right?' she asked, her rosy face entirely concentrated on Vanessa.

'I was twenty-one,' Vanessa admitted.

Lizzie shook her head in amazement, as though Vanessa had admitted to being sent up chimneys in childhood.

'I suppose we grew apart,' Vanessa ventured hopefully.

'Well yeah,' Lizzie conceded. 'Of course you did once he realised you were like this powerful woman. He married a girl, didn't he?'

Vanessa could see that Lizzie was leading her to some conclusion, but she was uncertain what it might be. She smiled anxiously. Lizzie rolled her eyes, but it was at Liam rather than Vanessa.

'He didn't leave because he was tired of you, Vanessa, he left because he was frightened of you,' she said. 'Terrified. You're a mother, a woman – I've got this brilliant book about it. You can borrow it if you like.'

From what Lizzie said, Vanessa gleaned that she took an equal interest in Cleo's relationship with her boyfriend of sorts, Mick. Mick worked for an insurance company and was nearly twenty years younger than Cleo. Cleo was always very rude about him. According to her he reproduced much of the stolid pomposity of her ex-husband.

'But she says he's company,' Lizzie told Vanessa, with a kind of sympathetic disgust. 'She says when you get to her age that's what counts.'

'Well, it's nice to have,' Vanessa said, a little wistfully.

'I suppose so,' said Lizzie. 'I suppose a lot of women Cleo's age don't have anyone.'

'Look at me for a start,' laughed Vanessa self-consciously. Lizzie's face contorted in dismay.

'But you're not old,' she exclaimed. 'You're years younger than Cleo!'

Vanessa smiled, unconsciously stroking her waist. 'Don't let her hear you say that,' she advised, more seriously than not.

Lizzie's own boyfriend, Richard, occasionally appeared to pick her up after work. His parents were wealthy, and he drove a Lancia which they had given him for his eighteenth birthday, ostentatiously parking it where Vanessa and Cleo could see it from the shop. When no parking spaces were available nearby, he took care to introduce the car into conversation. Vanessa and Cleo agreed that Richard was not nearly good enough for Lizzie. His ready smile had all the self-regarding charm of a six-year-old's, completely unsupported by charisma.

'And he's got no neck,' Cleo observed.

It was seldom now that Cleo and Vanessa had the opportunity to discuss such matters. With the advent of Lizzie, they had begun to work staggered shifts. It was strange to be deprived of each other's company after so long together, but in this respect, Lizzie's curiosity proved invaluable. Each could rely on her to supply exhaustive news of the other. In this way, Cleo learned the details of Vanessa's post-Liam furnishing decisions, while Vanessa heard all the vacillations attending Cleo's plans to join a plush health club which had opened a few doors down from the shop.

'I told her that she really should,' Lizzie said to Vanessa, during a discussion about the high membership fee.

'But she won't keep it up,' Vanessa protested. 'I know Cleo.'

Lizzie fiddled with a tray of amber rings she'd been

cleaning. 'But if you'd spent all that money it'd make you go, wouldn't it?'

'That's the idea, I suppose,' Vanessa said. Lizzie smiled at her, tried on a ring.

'It's all right for you, you don't have to worry about exercise and stuff.' She replaced the ring, musing. 'I mean, I don't blame Cleo,' she said warmly. 'I said to her – it must be really easy to let yourself go.'

Shortly after this conversation, Lizzie informed Vanessa that Cleo had taken the plunge and joined the club. So far, she was attending religiously after work.

'Good for her,' Vanessa said.

'Well, I don't know,' Lizzie mused. 'I think she might be getting a bit obsessive about it.' Her clear hazel eyes were wide with concern. 'I think it's Mick, to be honest.'

'Really?' asked Vanessa, carefully neutral. 'Why?'

Lizzie tucked her hair behind her ears and leaned across the counter. 'I mean, Cleo's always really cheerful and everything, except when she's depressed, but she talks about her age all the time, like she's really ancient or something. I think he's undermining her confidence.'

Vanessa, who was writing out price tags, said that she wouldn't be at all surprised. Cleo could often be her own worst enemy.

'But you mustn't take her seriously,' she advised Lizzie. 'Half the time she just says things for effect.'

'That's a genius jumper,' Lizzie remarked, catching her by the sleeve.

Vanessa looked down at herself, surprised. 'Do you like it?' she asked. Since she and Liam had parted, no one commented on her appearance except when Cleo asked her if she was feeling ill.

'It's fab,' Lizzie exclaimed, fingering the cuff.

'It's only a cheapie,' Vanessa told her. 'You could get one yourself if you like.'

Lizzie was wearing her new jumper when Vanessa was next in the shop. She had even taken Vanessa's advice that the black would be too severe on her, and had bought it in a heathery blue. She announced herself delighted with the result.

'Richard says I look like a librarian, though,' Lizzie said, surveying herself with satisfaction. 'He likes anything you can see, you know, my cleavage in.'

'That's men all over,' said Vanessa.

'Cleo says I should show everything while I can,' Lizzie told her. 'She says I'll have long enough for camouflage. Like the stuff she wears, she means.'

'Expensive camouflage,' remarked Vanessa, thinking of Cleo's designer layers. She had never had the bravery to burn so brightly herself.

'I told her she doesn't need to cover herself up all the time,' said Lizzie. 'I mean, not if she keeps going to the gym. She could be really glamorous if she tried.'

'Did you say that to her?' asked Vanessa, appalled.

'Yeah,' said Lizzie blithely. 'You can say anything to Cleo, can't you? That's what's great about her. She's so straight-forward.'

The following week, Vanessa was unsurprised to hear that things were still going badly between Cleo and Mick. Lizzie stressed that she was reading between the lines, since

Cleo had said nothing so bald, but it seemed clear from the way she had suddenly taken to piling on make-up and dressing in a way that was frankly a bit too young for her.

'It's a shame,' said Lizzie. 'Cleo's got such a fantastic personality and everything. You'd think she'd find someone really nice.'

'She frightens men off,' Vanessa told her. 'That's what Liam always said. She'd have your balls for breakfast.'

Lizzie grinned. 'That's funny—'

'Why?' asked Vanessa.

'Oh, nothing really. I mean, I don't think it's even true,' Lizzie assured her.

'What isn't?'

'Nothing,' Lizzie maintained. 'Just, you know. I'm sure you're right. I mean, I think she's fantastic, but I could see how Cleo would frighten men off. I mean that's probably why she says it.'

'What does she say?' asked Vanessa, smoothing her hair.

'That men are frightened by you,' confessed Lizzie. 'Funny, isn't it? She says it's because you can't sort of move on, from Liam I mean.' Consolingly, she added, 'Richard thinks you're gorgeous, by the way.'

Once the Christmas stock arrived, the current of business swept all three of them along so swiftly that conversation of any substance became impossible. A range of luridly naive Mexican plastics procured by Cleo proved ridiculously popular and for the first time, Quelque Chose took telephone orders. Also for the first time, there wasn't a thing in the shop, bar a card or two, which Cleo wouldn't happily have had in her own house. She and Mick had booked a flight to the Bahamas straight after Christmas, and there was no doubt that all should have been well in her world. But she'd drifted into one of her low patches. Vanessa alerted Lizzie to this when she reported that Cleo had snapped at her in response to a question about some novelty hot water bottles. Even at the memory, the girl's mobile face contracted as though from a blow.

'It just happens from time to time, that's all,' Vanessa counselled. 'I'm afraid you just have to keep your head down and wait for it to pass. She doesn't mean anything by it.'

'But that's terrible,' Lizzie objected. 'If she was getting headaches all the time she'd go to the doctor, wouldn't she?'

Lizzie brought the subject up again over lunch, snatched at the counter because of customers. She had forgotten to tell Vanessa that Cleo had stopped going to the gym.

'I told you it'd be a nine-day wonder,' Vanessa said. 'I know Cleo.'

'I just think Cleo's got as much of a right to be happy as anybody,' maintained Lizzie. She seemed quite distressed.

Vanessa rejected the crust of her prawn sandwich. 'Well, she is really,' she said reassuringly.

She herself had never felt better. Stung by Cleo's reported opinion of her effect on men, she had put a personal ad in the *Sunday Times*, and was several meetings into a liaison with an unexpectedly dashing surveyor. She had also, encouraged by Lizzie, sent off for application forms for a fashion and technology foundation course at a local college. Lizzie was confident that Vanessa would be awarded a place, although Vanessa had her doubts. And she was concerned about asking Cleo for a reference.

'It seems a bit disloyal,' she confided to Lizzie.

'You're joking,' Lizzie exclaimed. 'Cleo'll be thrilled for you. Just because she's in a bit of a rut doesn't mean she'll stand in your way.'

Emboldened, Vanessa decided to approach Cleo when they were next in the shop together. It was the week before Christmas, and Vanessa had agreed to work extra days.

'All hands on deck, doll,' Cleo greeted her when she arrived. She was replenishing baskets with wooden tree ornaments. It had been weeks since Vanessa and Cleo had seen each other for more than a few minutes, and Vanessa privately thought that Cleo looked dreadful. From Lizzie, she had heard all about the argument Cleo had provoked with Mick, during which they had decided to cancel their holiday in the Bahamas.

'I mean, I think it's a good thing really,' Lizzie said at the time, 'because he's not good enough for her. He contributes to her low self-esteem. She knows that's what I think'.

Across the shop, Lizzie gave Vanessa an eager smile and a thumbs-up sign. Her pulse leaping, Vanessa pulled out the college application forms from her bag. She asked Cleo to be her referee. Cleo scanned the papers, her eyebrows framing contempt.

'Well, this is news,' she said. Her mouth was set into a stripe of magenta lipstick.

'Of course I'd have to cut my hours down if I get in,' Vanessa gabbled. 'I mean, if that's all right with you, Cleo. If you wanted to get somebody else I'd quite understand. Someone more permanent, I mean.'

'Don't be silly, darling,' said Cleo. 'You know that there'll always be a place for you here.' She handed back the papers.

'I told you she'd be brilliant about it,' Lizzie exclaimed. She turned to Cleo. 'This is just so cool of you.'

Cleo made no further mention of the reference as the three of them worked through Christmas week. Now that she was accustomed to Lizzie's company, Vanessa found it strange to be with Cleo again. Cleo had put herself on a punishing diet, and was quite literally shrunken. But it wasn't just an alteration in her physical presence that struck Vanessa. Compared to Lizzie's vivid evocations of her, Cleo seemed faded, as though it was the original that had lost definition through being copied. The only time she was stirred into her former expansiveness was when a customer asked if they stocked pot-pourri.

'Over my dead fucking body,' she declared, to Vanessa's private relief.

Of course they were all run ragged, Vanessa reminded herself, and none more than Cleo. They had extended closing time until nine o'clock for the last three days.

'Never mind, girls,' exhorted Cleo wearily. They were slumped against the counter, gathering their energies. It was Christmas Eve. 'This time next week the whole hideous business will be over, thank Christ.'

Vanessa admitted that she was actually looking forward to Christmas. She always did. She told Cleo and Lizzie about her plans for the holidays, and her progress with the surveyor, whose name was Mark. Lizzie's attention was rapt.

'It's so romantic,' she said yearningly. 'I wish Richard was like that.'

'He sounds divine,' conceded Cleo, folding silk pyjamas. 'But don't go falling head over heels.'

Vanessa assured her that they were taking their time. 'I'm hardly a schoolgirl,' she said.

'But you're inclined to be naive,' Cleo admonished her magisterially.

'When I need your advice, I'll ask for it, thank you very much,' Vanessa told her, whisking away to deter a woman who was disordering a pile of scarves. Cleo looked as though she had taken a step and missed a stair.

Some hours later, Cleo brought a customer to the till with a woollen wrap she had selected for her.

'Have you tried the green one?' Vanessa asked as she rang it up. One of the books that Lizzie had lent her had led her to the conclusion that she should have more confidence in her own good taste. The woman turned to Cleo. Cleo had counselled a pattern that was predominantly brown. Unable to resist, Vanessa added, 'I think the green would do more for your complexion.'

'Oh yeah, definitely,' said Lizzie, in passing.

The customer asked to see the green wrap. Lizzie brought it for her and the woman agreed that it would be more suitable. Vanessa could see that Cleo was simmering, but a man confronted her with an impatient question about a phone order and the moment retreated, unignited.

As soon as the last customer had been wished a merry Christmas and Lizzie had bolted the door, Cleo blew. It was nothing Vanessa hadn't withstood before. In fact, she had been more or less expecting it. She remained silent, waiting for the storm to pass as Cleo berated her for her lack of professionalism, lamented her own folly for always being too good-hearted and caring too much, and shook her fist at God for the general difficulty of her life. Lizzie watched in frozen amazement, terrified to draw attention to herself. This worked until Cleo was reaching the dregs of her outrage, and seeking fresh impetus. She pointed a melo-dramatic finger, adorned with a heavy pewter ring.

'And you—' she started, drawing a bead on Lizzie, but Vanessa intervened.

'Oh Cleo,' she said quietly. 'Honestly. Grow up.'

Cleo withdrew her finger. Lizzie scuttled out of range and got her coat. Vanessa began to cash up, in silence. Without looking at her, Cleo joined in.

'Erm, merry Christmas,' said Lizzie cautiously. She was holding out two small boxes, identically wrapped in silver paper. Envelopes were trapped beneath silver ribbon. 'It's nothing much,' she apologised, extending one of the boxes to Cleo on her palm, as though feeding an animal of uncer-tain temperament. Cleo made a large, inclusive gesture.

'Oh darling,' she exclaimed. 'You make me feel like a fucking monster!'

'Thank you,' added Vanessa.

They both made much of unwrapping the boxes and sniff-ing the vials of essential oils contained within.

'Eau de Valium, I hope,' said Vanessa, wafting the small blue bottle beneath her nose.

'It's rejuvenating,' Lizzie explained. 'And yours is stimu-lating,' she told Vanessa.

Earlier in the day, Cleo had told Lizzie to choose her favourite item in the shop worth around twenty pounds, without mark-up. Lizzie had prudently chosen a Japanese origami lampshade priced at eighteen pounds, insisting that it was something she really wanted. She hoisted the box with an apologetic smile.

'Thanks again,' she said.

'My pleasure,' Cleo assured her.

Lizzie wished them another subdued merry Christmas and left. Cleo gave a laden sigh.

'Oh Christ,' she said. Vanessa said nothing. With her black pen, she continued to make neat towers of figures on a damaged sheet of wrapping paper. Every time Cleo drew a breath indicative of her desire to speak, Vanessa dotted her pen at the sums and mouthed numbers on an indrawn breath, as though calculating.

As they finished cashing up, Cleo handed Vanessa a sealed envelope. This was a surprise, as they had a policy of never exchanging Christmas cards or presents.

'Don't worry, darling, it isn't a book token,' Cleo said, reading her expression. 'It's the reference for your thingummy.'

Disarmed, Vanessa thanked her. Cleo brusquely said that it had only taken her a few minutes.

'There's not that much to say about you, doll,' she retorted. Then, seeing Vanessa's anxiety she added, 'But it's all good, don't worry.'

Cleo disappeared into the back to make them a cup of coffee. Using the counter as a shield, Vanessa prised open the envelope containing the reference. Hot with dread, she unfolded the paper and furtively scanned the paragraph of typescript.

She read: 'Vanessa Wilson has been assistant manager of my shop for the last fifteen years. During that time, she has shown herself to be loyal, competent and efficient. Her opinions about stock are always well worth listening to, particularly clothing stock. She has an impeccable sense of style – some would say a better sense of style than mine! –'

Cleo was returning with the coffee. As she fumbled to replace the sheet of paper, Vanessa caught the phrases 'invaluable asset to Quelque Chose', 'visual flair' and 'desperately sorry to see her go' amid the print.

Cleo had brought her a biscuit. Although she didn't want one, Vanessa ate it. Cleo always enjoyed watching people eat when she was on a diet. Distractedly, Cleo sniffed at the little bottle of oil Lizzie had given her.

'Rejuvenating,' she said, musingly.

'Lovely Lizzie,' smiled Vanessa.

'Yes,' Cleo sighed. 'Lovely Lizzie.'

'You know,' said Vanessa with some difficulty, brushing crumbs from her lap, 'I feel very guilty about the course and everything. Leaving you in the lurch.'

Cleo waved her away contemptuously. 'Forget it,' she said. 'To tell you the truth, doll, I've been thinking about closing anyway.'

Vanessa lowered her mug. She couldn't have been more shocked. 'What on earth for? You're making a bomb.'

Cleo put a weary hand to her face, sighed. 'But it's not making me happy,' she said, in the tones of a small girl. Careless of her kohl, she swiped at her eyes as though they had made her angry.

'Oh Cleo,' Vanessa said.

She attended sympathetically as Cleo gave a few gulps, then wept.

'I'm sorry I'm such a dreary old cow,' she apologised, accepting a fresh tissue from the pack Vanessa always kept in her purse.

'You're worn out,' Vanessa told her.

'I know I am. I don't know what's wrong with me. Ever since we started doing well, it's like . . . I don't know. I feel like the stuffing's gone out of me.' Cleo lit a cigarette and took a quavering drag. 'Not all at once. Bit by bit, like there's a leech on me or something. Fuck it. Maybe I should have some tests done.'

'It's fear of success,' said Vanessa.

'Is it?' Cleo asked.

'It's not uncommon,' Vanessa reassured her. 'Women get it all the time. It's in this book Lizzie lent me. I'll lend it to you if you like.'

Cleo exhaled. 'That's another thing,' she said, her eyes gazing into distant self-reproach. 'I can't even be nice about Lizzie.'

'Lovely Lizzie,' Vanessa sighed.

'Yes,' said Cleo wanly. 'Disgusting, isn't it? Lovely Lizzie. All she wants to do is help.'

Most Wanted

My parents, engrossed by other matters, failed to realise that my sister had turned into a thief. I was fourteen and inundated by sex, but even I had noticed something. Trivial objects disappeared, and she was lurking and secretive. Still, her felonies didn't loom large until agencies beyond the family brought them harshly to light. My sister, by the way, was eight at the time. You can draw your own conclusions about the significant gap in our ages.

The first incident occurred when Dad picked Michelle up from a friend's house. My dad, while a willing and biddable chauffeur, was not the favourite for transactions of the collecting-from-a-friend's-house variety. No dads were particularly good at this, I had noticed. When confronted by friends' mothers, they became nervy and monosyllabic, as

though their paternal powers were weakened by the ema-
nations of a rival home, like Superman by kryptonite. They
were even worse when it was another dad who greeted
them at the door. Then, both parties seemed likely to be
overwhelmed entirely out of existence by mutual embarrassment. Mums were better. They could be relied upon to
roll their eyes with their counterparts in pantomimed sympathy at your shortcomings, while taking an interest in your
hurried account of the preceding social occasion, all the
time conducting a shrewd inventory of the kit trailing
behind you and rustling up stray items of clothing. Their
mild social betrayal with other mothers ('You don't fancy
keeping her then?') was compensated for by the close attention paid to the full account of your activities during the
drive back home. Our dad fell very short on this score, and
always had. Even when we were small he seldom exhibited
the meagre responses necessary to maintain a belief in his
attention. ('A balloon?' 'Was it?' 'A *blue* balloon?')

Of course I had reached an age at which Dad's lack of
interest had transformed itself into a blessing, but my sister
still expected more. So she must have been disappointed to
see him standing at the door, wanly, leaving Mrs Church to
do the final check on possessions which in more ideal cir-
cumstances would have been conducted by our mother. It
was in a spirit of efficiency and not malice that Mrs Church,
frisking a swimming bag, stumbled upon her own daughter's
tube of Sweet Missy shower gel. And it was her daughter,
Alison, who first wailed that my sister had stolen it. Even
then, if my mum had been there, she could have transformed this possible crime into something foolish but

redeemable. Instead of which, my dad goaded Michelle into an extravagant and finally tearful apology, slapped her legs in front of Alison and Mrs Church, and carted her back to the car in disgrace.

For the first time in months, Michelle had got Dad's full attention, and it continued into a remarkably sullen family tea. I was sullen because a recent laxity in the family routine meant I could generally slope off to my room with a pot of yoghurt and a jam doorstep without having to sit round a table, my dad and sister were sullen in the aftermath of her theft, and my mother was sullen for her own reasons.

'I don't understand,' Dad reiterated, as Mum doled out bloodless mounds of shepherd's pie. 'We've always given you pocket money.'

My sister poured a long wound of ketchup over the surface of her food and stirred it into the mashed potato, tinting it pink.

'If you wanted anything you could have asked for it. Eat that properly.'

'What's she done?' I asked, perking up. I was told the full story. Mum took a deep, roaming breath.

'I think we've heard enough about it for now,' she said, and told Michelle she could leave the meat and just eat the potato.

That night, our parents had a long, hopeless row that flared up over the nine o'clock news and continued in loops of reproach into the small hours. I fell asleep to the muffled syncopation of their argument coming through my bedroom wall. It was becoming too familiar to interrupt my sleep and in any case I was preoccupied by other demands. These were in the form of urges, conjured by a boy in my class called Gary, but currently self-satisfied. I went round to his house after school and we discussed sex, or more accurately, masturbation, with great enthusiasm and not a stroke of physical contact. While our classmates roiled in saliva and melodramatics, I prided myself on the more measured and serious way in which we were advancing our carnal knowledge. That day, indeed, I had drawn Gary a diagram of the female genitals and explained to him their relative areas of sensitivity. He had asked interested questions and reciprocated with surprising information about the penis and its ways.

Although there was an idea of Gary which helped me in my nightly explorations of my own sexual equipment, it tallied remarkably little with the actual Gary who sprawled daily on the carpet next to me, bony in his grey school pullover and pungent with a boyish smell of sweat and stale biscuits. In some way, I thought, the practical side of our relationship would commence once we had become thoroughly grounded in the theory. But as yet, our knowledge was far from extensive.

For most of a week, Michelle mimed careful good behaviour with any potentially incriminating trace of her personality removed. We had to undergo a number of family meals, enjoyed by no one. At one of them, Mum suggested that Alison Church be invited for tea. Dad didn't attempt a comment, knowing it had never been his place to initiate such transactions. But Michelle seemed slightly heartened by the suggestion, and ate most of her poached egg.

Mum must have done the necessary in the way of approaching Mrs Church because a couple of days later Alison was there when I got home from Gary's. She and my sister were installed at the kitchen table, eating tinned mandarin oranges and giggling helplessly. Alison was apparently doing something amusing involving a mandarin segment and her tongue, but she quickly closed her mouth once I approached. She got on my nerves, and she was sufficiently aware of the fact to be frightened of me. I let the tap run as cold as possible, and made lemon squash.

'Where's Mum?' I asked them.

'Out. Dad's watching telly.' Once she had said this, Michelle whispered something to Alison and they started giggling again. I left them to it and went upstairs. On my way I walked past the living room, where Dad was watching a favourite game show. He barely acknowledged me when I greeted him. The room, I noticed, was a mess. This gave unexpected ammunition to the campaign I was waging for the right to clean (or not) my own room. I concluded that Mum must have been in a hurry when she went out, because the disorder was unusual. Dad never cleaned, but as far as I could see nor did he contribute to making things untidy, unlike me and Michelle. Of course the by-product of his existence was a certain amount of housework since he ate and wore clothes, but this was not the sort of housework liable to provoke Mum's irritation. It hadn't been until recently, anyway.

'Where's Mum?' I asked.

'You'd better ask her,' Dad said, with more than a suggestion of self-pity.

'Well I can't, can I?' I pointed out, irresistibly. He ignored me and concentrated on the TV. I thundered upstairs, only to be driven out about an hour later by the sound of my sister howling on the way to her bedroom, chased by futile cries of 'You come back here, madam!' from Dad. I went into her room, which was next door to mine. It was in fact the only real alternative bedroom in the house, but a year before I had insisted on privacy, so the box-room had become my room, with a couple of feet to spare around the single bed. Our previous room, now solely Michelle's, retained bunkbeds and many of my childhood possessions, bequeathed to her. I avoided going in there much.

Michelle was on the top bunk, sobbing in a shuddering, automatic way. I approached her carefully. Her knobbled little legs hung over the edge of the bed, covered in white socks, grubby on the soles. I poked my forefingers through the lacy pattern of the socks, to the cold skin beneath. Michelle was always cold. The flesh on her legs above her socks was mottled and forlorn.

'What've you done now?' I asked her. She yanked her legs back on to the bed and twisted unforthcomingly on to her stomach.

'All right, I'm not bothered.' I wandered over to the toy stable I had received on my ninth birthday and toyed with a rigid-legged pony, his mane long ago hacked off in a misguided hairdressing experiment.

'It isn't fair,' she informed me.

'Have you been nicking things again?'

'No! Alison said I could lend it.'

'Borrow it,' I corrected. 'What?'

'Her Jungle puzzle.'

Dad, still smarting from the ignominious fruits of Mrs
Church's random search, had insisted that Alison go through
a checklist of her possessions before leaving our house.
Upon finding herself short of her Jungle puzzle she had
informed my father, who had then practically strip-searched
Michelle, notwithstanding Mrs Church's objections that
Alison had probably left the silly thing at home. The silly
thing quickly came to light, stuffed under Michelle's jumper.
It was returned to Alison, Mrs Church was fulsomely apologised to, and Michelle's knickers were pulled down and
her bottom resoundingly slapped in full view of her guest.
She had of course howled. I couldn't blame her for being
upset.

'Why'd you take it?' I asked her. Ineffectually, she palmed
tear-soaked snakes of hair from her face.

'I did-errrrrn't,' she wailed insistently, on an ascending
scale.

Much later, I heard Mum come in, followed from room
to room by Dad's angry recounting of the crime. Before he
could get to the end, there was the sound of Mum's tread on
the stairs. I popped my head out. She was eating a Scotch
egg, which deflated the drama of the situation.

'Just a sec.' The light was still on in Michelle's room.
She went in, and switched it off.

'Fast asleep.'

Mum took another hungry bite of Scotch egg. We
regarded each other. She had bright orange crumbs round
her mouth and seemed to be in a good mood. I was struck
by the surprising thought that she had once been my age.

'Night then.' I retreated behind my door.

The next day Dad made Michelle write out a couple of signs in felt tip which said 'I am a thief', and then forced her to sellotape one to the wall above her bed and the other above her desk. Gary was playing football that afternoon so I went straight home from school. As soon as I walked into the kitchen, the atmosphere collected around me. A phone call had been received, from Millbank Junior.

Upstairs, Mum was conducting a search of Michelle's room in order to locate the fourteen library books, scandalously overdue, which had been signed out in her name. So far, the search had unearthed a total of twenty-three books with the Millbank Junior library stamp, leading to the obvious suspicion that some of them (there were a lot of *Secret Sevens*) had left the premises without benefit of signature. Mum was less outraged by this than by the incidental discovery of several weeks' worth of Michelle's school lunches, tucked away in obscure crevices among her toys and in varying states of putrefaction. Michelle was unable to explain why she hadn't at least thrown the unwanted lunches out. As Mum gingerly pincered them into a bin liner I noted, without remark, that each lunch was missing its statutory wrapped chocolate biscuit. Michelle watched everything from her bed, sobbing shallowly. Mum got her a wet flannel and wiped her face for her.

'We won't tell your dad about this,' she said, very quietly, as though the words weighed too much to be spoken normally. Mum hugged Michelle, who didn't resist. Then she tore down the 'I am a thief' signs and put them in the bin.

When we all shared our overcooked, cottony roast

chicken a few hours later, we passed things politely and Michelle made squash for everyone without moaning. The conversation was as fragile as blowing bubbles. Dad, naturally, was suspicious, but as he had no grounds to make an accusation he restricted himself to meaning looks. I departed to my homework with some relief.

Gary and I were undergoing a crisis. Our arrangement, for months so admirable and mutually rewarding, had been breached by him attempting to kiss me. If I had had some warning, I would have had time to marshal a different set of instincts, but when his hot mouth had landed inaccurately on mine I bucked away in reflex astonishment that must have appeared to him as repulsion. I didn't know for sure, because we couldn't talk about it. We couldn't talk at all since it had happened, about anything. I devised lengthy, lucid speeches and failed to deliver them. It wasn't that I didn't want him to kiss me, I just wanted sufficient notice so that I could participate in it. Then, no more than a week later, I saw him snogging Caroline Meadows in the bus queue. They were mauling each other avidly, oblivious of onlookers. All my afternoons with Gary were replaced by a low, sickly weight in my stomach. I saw it entirely. He was probably deploying all the knowledge gleaned from me to her benefit, and his. That I had thought a boy might value conversation, even conversation about sex, over sex itself suddenly coagulated into the most abject stupidity.

This trauma inhibited sleep and generally dulled my awareness of a world beyond my suffering. The idiosyncrasies of my bedroom ceiling took on an unconsidered familiarity, as I glassily re-ran the story of Gary and me each night after tea, with a variety of never to be realised endings. Well into the second week of this, Mum came into my room, so quietly that I didn't reprimand her for failing to knock. I adjusted my focus, nervous that she was about to intervene with some inadequate attempt at consolation.

She balanced on the edge of my bed.

'I wanted to talk to you because you're old enough to understand things.'

This was immediately dreadful, and it got worse. She was leaving Dad. They were splitting up. They loved us, but they didn't love each other any more. I'd understand when I was older. They both deserved to be happy. She was still a young woman, by today's standards. There was a new friend she wanted me to meet. Things often turned out for the best, I'd see.

'Does Dad know?'

'Yes.'

I yawned, and said nothing. She tried to touch me but I glared the impulse away.

'What about us?'

'We'll still be a family.'

She hadn't spoken to Michelle. I wondered if she had told me hoping, as when she had explained the facts of life, that I would disseminate the information downwards. I was determined to let her do her own dirty work on this one. I got up and went downstairs, leaving her sitting on the bed.

It seemed incredible that Dad still existed, watching the telly with a cup of tea next to his feet. The tea had gone cold; I could see the pearly scum on its surface. I gently asked him if he wanted another cup. He declined, as embarrassed as me. I was dawdling out when he said,

'Your sister's in trouble again.'

He had a letter from the school, open on his lap. This time she was under suspicion of taking a flute from the music room. She played the violin, not the flute. Dad seemed surprisingly resigned, although the instrument was worth well over a hundred pounds. Michelle was out at gymnastics. I offered to help him search her room.

Mum insisted on helping as well, although I told her that we could manage without her. So the three of us set to it, silently. I was the first to strike lucky, happening on the end piece of the flute shoved down the chimney of my old doll's house. A few minutes later, Dad found the other two pieces. They were tucked beneath a pile of unloved dolls whose limbs, in attitudes of stiff dismay, had been scribbled on with felt pen. He sat on the bed and screwed together the dismembered instrument.

'Alison Church plays the flute,' I told him. I remembered her carrying the little oblong case, rivalry between her and Michelle about the relative difficulties of flute and violin.

'Poor kid,' said Dad.

'It wasn't Alison's she took.'

'I meant Michelle.'

He pressed the keys, which made a dull, felt-muffled click. The front door went, slamming in the way Michelle got shouted at for. I heard Michelle go into the living room and put the TV on. Dad made a sound, something liquid and involuntary. He drew it back into himself, but it carried on. Mum put her hand out to his face. I expected him to shake it off, wanted him to, but he let her hand rest. I went downstairs, banging, bursting to tell Michelle that she was in big trouble, to see her face redden and the tears start. She was curled on the settee in her gymnastics leotard, staring at the telly. She looked just like she always did, holding her icy feet to warm them. She looked small.

'This is all your fault,' I said, and I meant it, but she didn't hear me over the TV. So I went into the front room instead, and found a book to read. None of it had anything to do with me any more.

Lost

Jodie's mother, Mel, often told her that she had been an accident. When Jodie was smaller this had had associations with ambulances, or plasters on knees, but now she knew that it had to do with sex. Quite what, she wasn't old enough to guess, although Mel would have told her if she'd asked. She didn't ask, because she didn't quite want to know. It might be bad. Anyway. Auntie Sharon wouldn't have told her and she was the only one left to tell.

Mel had rung Sharon from motorway services on a Sunday. They were already on their way. Before she opened the door, Sharon knew that something was up, but when she saw them she realised that it was something more than usual. Mel herself looked awful, her body bloated by an extra stone but her face drawn and older under her make-up. Jodie was carefully dressed. Her hair, which had a mind of its own, had obviously been tamed in the car just before they got out. Her mother's spit glistened in her hairline.

The little girl smiled at Sharon a little tightly. The three of them didn't see each other very often. Sharon, after pouring a glass of orange juice, suggested that Jodie play with the things on the chest of drawers in her bedroom while she and Mel had a cup of coffee. Jodie took the hint.

Auntie Sharon had a good collection of things on her chest of drawers, including a jewellery box and several cats made out of painted wood and china, so Jodie got to work rearranging them, telling herself a story about the cats in her head. She was used to playing quietly, especially lately. The request brought a heavy dread to her stomach, because she knew that her mum was talking about That. But on the whole she preferred being sent to play quietly to staying in the same room. Then, she had to pretend that she couldn't hear the low confidences which intensified the further she moved away, then stopped completely as soon as she approached, only to be told to go away again. When she did, Mel's voice started behind her once more, like it was playing a game of Grandmother's Footsteps. It was impossible not to hear some of what was said. None of it was nice.

Sharon slept in the spare room the first night, leaving her double bed for Mel and Jodie. She had overriden Mel's suggestion that they put Jodie down in the single and share the double themselves. The prospect of sharing with her sister alarmed her. Already, after less than seven hours together, she felt irritated raw, the way skin is irritated by contact unsympathetic to its tenderness. She needed to be alone in the bed, away from the abrasion of Mel's distress. Silence, like a salve.

Their mother was dead and their father was in a nursing home, a stranger to himself and the world. She was Mel's only sibling, and she would have to help her out.

The flat was quite small with three of them in it. Jodie was used to making herself small, but Mel wasn't. Jodie could see that Auntie Sharon was annoyed with Mel most of the time, and most annoyed when she tried to help. Mel went out one morning and brought some buns back for breakfast, as a treat she said, and Auntie Sharon nearly got angry. Jodie could feel it leaving her and filling the air, like cigarette smoke. Auntie Sharon said no thanks, that she tried not to eat crap, and spooned down a bowl of gravelly muesli as Jodie and Mel ate sweet pastry submerged under white icing. Jodie levered off the waxy cherry from the top and left it on her plate. The icing around its absence was stained pink, but didn't taste any different. Auntie Sharon surprised her by shooting out her hand and popping the abandoned cherry in her mouth.

'That's the best bit,' she said. Jodie giggled, although she could tell that Auntie Sharon was still angry underneath. Still chewing the cherry, Auntie Sharon went out into the kitchen and took a pill, like she did every morning. Not the same ones Mel took, bubbled behind the days of the week on a card like a little advent calendar. Auntie Sharon's were different. Happy pills, Jodie heard Mel call them.

They must have made Auntie Sharon happy on the inside.

It was on the fourth day that Sharon caught Mel making a phone call. A phone call to *him*, that is. It was one in the morning and Mel had slid out of bed, leaving her sleeping child, and gone to the phone. In the dark, so that Sharon wouldn't see an incriminating slice of light from the living-room door. But Sharon was awake, wakeful with resentment in the spare room. Although the words weren't clear through the wall, the music of conciliation was, its soft lifts and repetitions. Finally, there were tears, and Sharon knew that Mel would be going back. Her relief at the prospect of being alone left just enough room for exasperation at Mel's stupidity. Change the record, she thought. You stupid cow. She found it necessary to get up.

On That Day there was a bun for breakfast again. Sitting on the plate with the cherry in the middle like a clown's nose. No smile below it though, no eyes above. This time Mel hadn't bothered to buy one for Auntie Sharon, or even for herself. They were both smoking. Jodie levered off the cherry and offered it to Auntie Sharon, who said she didn't feel like it. Then Auntie Sharon looked across at Mel and Jodie's stomach knew that something was about to be said that she would want to push back into her mother's mouth. But it wasn't that bad in the end. Just that Mel was going back to see Him while Jodie had a little holiday with Auntie Sharon. Jodie didn't bother to remind her mother what she'd said about Him. She didn't like to be reminded. But the main thing was that Jodie wouldn't have to see Him as well. And having a little holiday with Auntie Sharon would probably be OK. She ate the bun. It might be the last for a while.

Just before Mel left, Jodie reminded her that she would need her swimming costume if she was going to be on holiday.

This made her mum and auntie laugh. Although they looked so different, their laughs were the same, like twins.

'Auntie Sharon will get you another one, chick,' said Mel. Then she tried to push a twenty-pound note into Auntie Sharon's hand but Auntie Sharon pulled her hands away and put them behind her back so that she couldn't. Mel put the money on the table and Auntie Sharon snatched it up and tried to give it back. This time it was Mel who pulled her hands away. They were getting cross with each other, although they were laughing at the same time.

'Go on,' said Mel. 'Please.' So Auntie Sharon gave in, rolling her eyes in resigned disapproval as Mel left the money on the table.

Jodie asked Sharon about her scar only once, on the day her mother left. As Sharon bent over her to say goodnight, the child reached up and silently traced its line across Sharon's forehead, her eyes following the straight path of her finger.

'Does it hurt?' she asked.

'No,' said Sharon, a door closing firmly in her voice. Jodie dropped her finger and settled down, content to sleep. Fleetingly, Sharon thought this was tact, then she remembered that Jodie had her own sense of what was normal, poor kid.

They walked everywhere. Auntie Sharon said it was good for you, like having honey in your tea instead of sugar. But Jodie knew that Auntie Sharon could drive because her mum had told her a story about when she had wanted to learn to drive and Auntie Sharon refused to teach her, even though she had already passed her own test. In the end, Mel had paid for driving lessons by saving up and saving up. It was a bit like Cinderella, Jodie thought. Mel hadn't bought any new clothes until the elbows of her jumpers all had holes in.

'Then she borrowed mine,' said Auntie Sharon, when Jodie told her this story. She meant it like a joke. She made them walk faster, though, so Jodie knew that it wasn't.

They were always very careful crossing roads.

Mel rang on Sunday night, using a voice with a bright, suspect shine to it. She told Sharon that everything was going great. Great was the word she used. Jodie chattered to her mother quite happily, then announced shortly after the call was over that she wanted to go to bed. It was an hour too early. When Sharon went to switch off the light she felt a pang at the small, self-contained arc Jodie made under the spare-room covers. They had swapped bedrooms after Mel had left. The radiator in the spare room didn't work and the air was icy compared to the warmth of the hall. She kissed Jodie's chilly cheek, but the child pretended to be asleep. Her eyelids convulsed minutely, betraying her.

The days they went swimming, Wednesdays, were the best. Auntie Sharon bought her a new swimming costume, just like Mel had said, and let her choose it herself. Jodie made sure that she paid for it with her mum's twenty pounds. There was enough money left to buy a pair of goggles as well, pink ones, and still some change. So they were really presents from Mel.

The pool had a wave machine, like the one they had been to once at home, before Mel met Him. There was another part for the grown-ups to swim in, up and down, keeping inside the lines, like colouring. Auntie Sharon only went in that if there was room in the line nearest the children's part, so she could watch her. Jodie had told her that she'd be all right, but she didn't listen. Afterwards they always had baked potatoes for tea, which were her favourite. Auntie Sharon showed Jodie how to roll up the empty skins and hold them between her forked fingers, pretending they were cigars. She said that's what she and Jodie's mum used to do when they were little. She surprised Jodie by waggling her rolled potato-skin cigar, squinting her eyes and talking in a funny American voice. The next week, Jodie did it too. That's what they always did, on Wednesdays.

When Mel skipped a Sunday night, Sharon rang instead. She intended to give her sister a piece of her mind about letting the kid down. *He* answered the phone, though, and said that Mel had gone out. He didn't even bother to be civil. Sharon didn't believe him about Mel being out, although she didn't argue the toss. She told Jodie that her mum would ring her tomorrow. Fortunately, Jodie was absorbed in a TV programme. And when Sharon did get hold of Mel, she withheld the piece of her mind. Her sister's voice had lost its lustre.

She shouldn't have let the other thoughts out into her head. Some of them must have escaped when she was asleep and marched along the hall like ants and up on to the pillow and climbed in through Auntie Sharon's ear. Or maybe they undid the scar on her forehead like a zip, and jumped straight into her brain.

Auntie Sharon said it as Jodie was handing in her books at the library desk.

'We'll have to think about school for you, madam.'

She said it a little loudly, so that the librarian could hear her and smile. It was the librarian they often saw, with crayoned eyebrows and a mole. She was very slow when she stamped your book, like the stamp was kissing the page goodbye and never wanted it to leave the library.

'After Christmas,' Auntie Sharon added. Jodie didn't say anything back. Her throat clenched. Not about school, although that was bad enough, but about Christmas. A little holiday, they'd said. Until Christmas was a long time. After Christmas was too long to even think past.

Mel didn't ring at the weekend. Sharon waited for Jodie to mention it but she didn't. Kids were very resilient.

She was putting the potatoes into the oven when it happened. It was a Wednesday. The child ran into the kitchen, her face bleached with panic. As her heart lurched, Sharon's sense of disaster was terrible, yet tainted with boredom, a dull fulfilment of expectation. A relief, almost. Oh no. At last. She froze as Jodie gasped her distress. She had been hanging their swimming stuff over the radiator to dry and couldn't find her swimming goggles. Sharon's wasted terror diverted itself into irritation.

'They probably dropped out when you were drying your hair,' Sharon told her, 'or you left them in the changing room. Someone will have handed them in.'

But what if they hadn't? Jodie asked, tears welling. What if the goggles had dropped out of her bag on the way home and nobody found them? Or what if someone had picked them up at the pool and decided to keep them for themselves, or mixed them up with their own goggles? Or stolen them?

'It's all right,' Sharon soothed her. 'I'll ring the pool and find out if they've been handed in.'

'But what if—'

'And if they haven't been—'

She had misjudged. If they haven't been reinforced the possibility of loss. Jodie's face shuddered ominously. Sharon caught the child by the shoulders and squatted to face her. It was like watching a bath reach capacity and tremble with the threat of overflowing, as she impotently spun the taps to stop it.

'Listen, listen, if they haven't been handed in I'll get you another pair.'

'It's not the same!' Jodie wailed, and cascaded into hysteria. She was breathless, consumed by grief, sobbing that it wasn't the same. Tears bowled down her face, already slick with them, the point of her chin dripping.

'Hey,' Sharon admonished her. 'Come on now. It's not worth getting upset, love.' She moved to hold her, more by determination than instinct. 'They're just crappy plastic.'

This was even worse. Jodie squealed and writhed and with an impatient spasm, batted Sharon away. 'I want my mum,' she blurted, and ran upstairs, choking on tears.

Sharon took her newspaper into the living room and closed the door. Let her cry herself out, she thought, reading the large page at the distance of her stiffened arms, using the paper as a prop to mask her anger, as though Jodie still stood in front of her. After all she'd done.

Jodie had a good memory. People always told her that. So she didn't have any trouble recalling the way to the swimming pool. It helped walking all the time with Auntie

Sharon. In cars, it was easy to dream and forget the way. Perhaps that was why Auntie Sharon didn't have one. But there was the street with the concrete posts at the end, covered with graffiti. Smell of pee. She walked slowly, scanning the ground, breathing through her mouth until she was past the smell.

It was possible that the pair of goggles could still be there. Anyone might think that they had been thrown away because they were broken and not have bothered to pick them up. They wouldn't see that the goggles were perfectly good. Excellent in fact. Crossing the road, then down to the end. Then the big road.

Getting no answer, Sharon waited outside the bathroom for a minute, until the absence of noise persuaded her to push open the door. It was empty, as perhaps she had known. But now she would have to act. Frantic, yet methodical, she searched under the bed and in her wardrobe, in case Jodie had decided to play a game.

It had happened.

It was already dark. People in the street turned round as she called out, but nowhere was there that green coat and straggle of hair. Sharon started to run, although she didn't know if she was running in the right direction. There was a toy shop down the road, just about to close. If Jodie was there, she bargained, she wouldn't even lose her temper with her. But the only children in the shop had parents attached.

In the junior library, she had the advantage of height to scan the assortment of heads dipped along the shelves. No Jodie.

She would murder her when she saw her. As long as she was OK. As long as nothing awful had happened. She imagined having to tell Mel. Or the police coming to Mel's door. Like they must have done. Oh God, oh God.

When Jodie was almost at the swimming pool she came to a large triangle of dead grass, divided by an unofficial path. Their short-cut. It was the one patch of dark, and it frightened her. But she would have to go, because she and Auntie Sharon had taken the short-cut on the way home. Then it had been light, and she had held Auntie Sharon's hand, stern and scratchy in a woolly glove. Now there were no edges to what she had to cross, just the complicated smell of trodden earth.

There was a man. She hadn't seen him because she was looking at the ground. She bumped into him, by accident.

The desk sergeant at the police station clearly thought Sharon was mad to begin with. She calmed herself, and used her best Radio Four voice. He promised to have a word with their area car to keep an eye out. She couldn't make a missing persons statement yet; it had been less than an hour. He advised her to go home and wait. If the worst happens, he started to say, then stopped himself, amending it to a promise to keep her informed of any developments. Sharon wanted to tell him that the worst had already happened. She wanted to scream its unfairness, that the worst could happen and be supplanted by a new worst.

That illumined moment of disaster, the horror of harming.

Jodie had to ring the bell to get back into the flat. She didn't have a key. It had taken much longer to get back from the swimming pool than she had estimated, perhaps because of the care with which she had searched, just to be sure. The goggles were definitely lost.

She wasn't worried until she had to ring the bell twice. But Auntie Sharon was there after the second ring. Her face looked strange, her scar standing out on her forehead, a purple line. Auntie Sharon must have been expecting a grown-up because her eyes had to drop to find Jodie. Then she grabbed her hard by the top of the arm and shouted. None of it was nice. It jumped out like something that had been waiting behind a curtain all along. Waiting until it could frighten her.

'Wicked girl.' Not as in good. As in witch. And more. About Mel, too, which made it worse. Fuck-up. Not fair. Always. Never. Towards the end Auntie Sharon tried to make her stop crying but she couldn't. She had to get a cold flannel for Jodie's face, which felt like someone else's face stuck over hers, hot and rubbery and uncomfortable.

From the bathroom, Jodie could hear Auntie Sharon talking to the police, and then to Him. She tried not to hear, but she could. Auntie Sharon couldn't cope. And she was supposed to be going back to work soon, so it made no difference anyway, she said in an arguing, final way. There would have to be another arrangement.

Jodie folded the flannel carefully, to be tidy.

'You can't expect to put it all on me,' she heard Auntie Sharon say. 'You can tell her. It isn't fair. I don't need this in my life, right?'

Four folds made it as small as it could get.

Cautious with each other, they ate their wizened baked potatoes from a tray in front of the TV, the abandonment of the table offered as a treat. Each left the inedibly rigid skins, without comment. Then Sharon let Jodie fall asleep watching TV next to her on the sofa, exhausted by misery and swimming. It occurred to Sharon then, supporting the child's matted head against her right shoulder, that she should have lied to Jodie about the goggles. She should have claimed the pool had rung her to say that they had been found, then replaced them with an identical pair. It was within her power to perform that miracle, but she had blown it. A mother would have known that, the magic of consoling. Even Mel would have known that.

When Sharon was ready to drop off, she braced herself to carry Jodie the short distance to the spare room. The weight of her took Sharon by surprise. Supporting the warm, massy body smelling of chlorine, the head lolling with its slight frown, Sharon tried not to associate it with anything beyond itself. Not the. Not. She was relieved when Jodie stirred, re-inhabiting her flesh. She blinked grumpily.

Something could come out of the dark and hit you, yet be hurt.

The spare room was freezing. Sharon retreated, then staggered with Jodie to her own room. She put her down in the double bed. Jodie's eyes opened, took in Sharon's face. Dreamily, she reached up beneath her dangling fringe to touch the scar.

'How did you get it?' she asked.

'I was in an accident,' Sharon told her.

'I was an accident,' said Jodie eagerly. Then, before Sharon could correct her, her eyelids fell and she slept, safe again in sleep.

Kiss Someone You Love

Afterwards, Suzy knew exactly when the trouble had started. She and Neil had just had sex, which was unusual on a weekday morning, but it was her fertile time. He got up and got ready for work while she rested in bed with her knees drawn up, willing his sperm to do its work. As she lay there, cradling her knees, she tried to think good thoughts. The first image to come was a grey kitten posed against bilious pink drapery, summoned from the side of a biscuit barrel once owned by her grandmother. Suzy dismissed it and reached for the smile of a baby, blinking and sated from a feed. It was a shame she hadn't had an orgasm; she'd read that it aided conception. Downstairs, there was a slack, tinny rattle as the letterbox disgorged the morning post.

Neil never picked up the post, even if he had to step over it on his way out to work. So it wasn't until she came down-stairs at nearly ten that Suzy retrieved the brown envelope from the mat, partly hidden by a flyer for a local decorator. She didn't have time to open it, since she was on her way out to a cleaning job. It wasn't from anyone she knew, anyway; that much she could tell from the writing on the address. She put it in her bag for later.

The cleaning was something Suzy and Neil argued about. Neil thought that she could be doing a better job, if she insisted on working at all. When they'd met, Suzy was an assistant at a private nursery, but it closed down about a year later and she made no attempts to get more of the same work, although the owner, Mrs Reeves, had offered to ask around for her. Instead, she had answered a card someone had put in a newsagent's window, looking for a cleaner. And from there, word of mouth had kept her in customers ever since. What Neil never accepted when they rowed about her cleaning was that Suzy liked the work. She enjoyed getting out and going into other people's houses. She even enjoyed the cleaning itself most of the time, because it was uplifting to see what a change she made to the state of things. And often there was company, because one of her employers worked from home and another was the wife of a wealthy husband and didn't work at all. It suited her.

'You're just a snob,' Suzy told Neil. 'You just don't like saying "my wife's a cleaner".'

'You're right, I bloody don't,' he retorted.

He didn't stop her, though. Neil wasn't really going to

stop her doing anything once she'd made up her mind about it. It was the same with them trying for a baby. He would have preferred them to wait a couple of years, but once Suzy told him she was ready now he took it in his stride.

Suzy could have read the letter on the bus to Eleanor and Greg's, but she was preoccupied by calculating delivery dates and it slipped her mind. Eleanor and Greg were a youngish couple she had had on her rota for nearly a year. Their house was a Victorian terrace on three floors, with a large kitchen extension at the back. It wasn't as modern as Suzy preferred, but she admired the way it had been decorated. Everything was well kept and mostly new, and there wasn't any clutter. This made her own job easier, since she never enjoyed dusting, but it also appealed to her taste. With the money, it was the kind of place she might have had herself.

As Suzy let herself into the house with her key a woman's voice – Eleanor's – shouted hello from the kitchen. Her heart dropped a beat in shock. She hadn't expected anyone to be home; both Eleanor and Greg worked.

'Come through,' Eleanor commanded in friendly tones.

Suzy normally communicated with the couple through a small red notebook left on the top of the fridge. This contained her weekly twenty-pound note, along with messages conveying any special requests, such as having a wipe round the skirting boards or scrubbing down the shower curtain. In return, Suzy entered requests for cleaning materials or receipts for cleaning materials already bought, for which she was always reimbursed. This procedure was the same for all her working couples. It would have been out of keeping for any of them to have included a note which strayed into the personal. So when Suzy entered the kitchen and found Eleanor seated at the table with her feet up on a chair, reading the paper, it was a shock to see the high, ripe dome of her stomach stretched beneath a matelot sweater.

'Hi Suzy,' Eleanor greeted her. 'You look well.'

'So do you,' said Suzy, genuinely. Eleanor fanned her fingers over her pregnancy with an apologetic grin.

'Huge, aren't I?' she sighed, proud. Eleanor was about five years older than her, Suzy guessed, in her early thirties, a small woman with precisely bobbed dark blonde hair and fair, rather dry skin. Although in their few dealings Eleanor had been nothing but pleasant, Suzy retained the impression that she was someone you wouldn't want to get on the wrong side of. She thought that Eleanor was a solicitor, although she couldn't remember for certain. A few of the people she cleaned for were.

'Another month to go,' Eleanor told her. 'Can you believe it? They say it's definitely not twins so he's going to be a giant. Or she.' She pulled a face and gestured to the mug she had in front of her. 'Would you like a cup of coffee?'

Suzy said that she'd better be getting on, but Eleanor insisted on getting up and making her a drink. Eleanor had never been particularly friendly before, but then, Suzy thought, she'd always been pressed for time when they had spoken. And it occurred to her, as she sat at the table and listened to Eleanor talk in detail about their choice of a home birth and techniques for the delivery, that Eleanor felt guilty about being in the house, apparently doing nothing, while she was there.

'Do you have any children?' Eleanor asked politely. Suzy said no. A jolt of rage at the question took her by surprise, like catching hold of a doorknob charged with static. What if she and Neil couldn't have children, and it was a sensitive area, or they'd had a baby and lost it? Not that it was, or they had, but people didn't think. She finished the coffee, which was unpleasantly strong. Then she washed both her and Eleanor's mugs at the sink, despite Eleanor's protests that they could go in the dishwasher.

'I'd better get on,' Suzy said. It was true, if she wanted to be finished by one.

She started on the bathroom. As she was scrubbing the taps on the wash-basin, Eleanor appeared at the door with her coat on and carrying her bag.

'I'm popping out,' she explained. 'We haven't got any-thing for the baby, it's terrible. With us both working I mean – it's the first chance I've had.'

Eleanor checked the contents of her large leather bag. It had a silky lining. 'I suppose people give you things, just before. My sister's giving us a cot and stuff.' Suzy nodded at this. Eleanor zipped up the bag. 'Is there anything you need? Bleach or anything?'

'I think you're all right,' Suzy told her. The door closed.

Her finger wrapped in a cloth, Suzy worried at dots of soap scum which had hardened in an arc on the light blue tile of the splashback. They contained tiny barbs of hair, the trace of Greg's shaken razor. This reminded Suzy of a woman she had heard or read about somewhere who had had a growth removed which turned out to contain hair and a fully grown tooth. Apparently it was the remnant of a twin that had never developed, which this woman had carried inside her obliviously all her life. The thought of the internal tangle of hair made Suzy feel queasy. In her dealings with other people's baths she always siphoned away their hairs without touching them, if at all possible. There was something about hair that disgusted her a little, something both dead and alive.

Thinking about hair made her want to tie her own hair back off her face, so she went downstairs for her bag and delved for an elastic. She had forgotten about the letter that had arrived that morning until she saw its corner poking out from under her purse. After she had pulled her hair into a ponytail, she took it out of her bag. The flap of the cheap brown envelope gave way with the first lift of her thumb, and Suzy removed a single folded sheet of white paper. It was almost filled with typewriter print, badly photocopied so that the chunk of text sat at an angle on the page, huddled against the right margin. It began:

> Kiss someone you love when you get this letter and make magic. With love all things are possible. This letter has been sent to you for good luck.

Realising what she was reading, Suzy skipped to the end of the page. A single line stood apart at the bottom. 'Remember, send no money. Do not ignore this letter. (It works.)' Beneath this, someone had added in a mixture of neatly printed lower case and capital letters, 'Please, Please don't through it away.'

Suzy replaced the sheet in the envelope and put it back in her bag. She was a little disappointed that it wasn't some-thing more exciting, although she couldn't imagine who might want to write to her out of the blue.

She didn't really believe in chain letters.

When Suzy next went to clean at Eleanor and Greg's, the restrained décor had been compromised by gaudy deposits of baby supplies, the fruits of Eleanor's shopping trip. Week by week, as the due date approached, corners and cup-boards continued to fill with bags of clothes and primary-coloured equipment, although Suzy found it strange that Eleanor hadn't prepared a nursery.

'It'll sleep with us to begin with,' Eleanor explained, unconcerned. 'And Greg can see to it when he gets some time off. If I try to clear out the spare room by myself I'll go pop.'

Suzy was relieved that Eleanor hadn't suggested she clear the spare room as one of her cleaning tasks. She was trying to avoid any heavy lifting, since she thought she might have conceived herself. She hadn't mentioned the possibility to Neil. It would get her own hopes up too much, giving the conception the solidity of a shared confidence. Her period was only a few days late and she'd had false alarms before. Although she could persuade herself that she felt different this time, it was too early for her body to be giving her reli-able signals. Still, it was difficult not to think about the baby, particularly when she saw Eleanor and imagined herself in seven months or so.

'All this stuff,' Eleanor lamented, moving a stack of bowls from a shelf to make room for an expensive-looking bottle steriliser. 'And it's useless after a couple of months.'

Suzy had a brief fantasy, which she quenched, of Eleanor giving her a pile of outgrown baby clothes. Eleanor had continued to be friendly, but Suzy knew that it was sheer excitement that made her confide her choices of name (Jack for a boy, Madeleine for a girl) and detail every twinge of her physical progress, while mere politeness prompted her brief questions about Suzy's own life.

There was a difference between being friendly and actually wanting someone for a friend.

Once her period was overdue by three weeks, Suzy bought two pregnancy tests, to be on the safe side. It was a Tuesday morning and she wasn't working until the afternoon. She hoovered tentatively as she waited for the wands to change colour. She liked the fact that the instructions called the stick you peed on a wand, suggesting magic. Although she was tempted to go and check the tests immediately for signs of transformation, Suzy forced herself to stay away by concentrating on the stair carpet, which showed a line of dust trapped at each junction where tread and riser met. Their hoover, unlike most of the ones she dealt with professionally, wasn't very powerful, so she had to gather up the long skeins of fluff and dirt with her fingers, disliking the sensation. With one stair left to go, Suzy rushed up to the bathroom. Each wand showed a definite blue stripe.

That night, she took Neil out to a pub near their house which did decent bar food. Neil enjoyed the novelty of them going out together in the middle of the week. He said that they should do it more often.

'We'd better do it while we can, then,' Suzy told him, putting down her knife and fork. 'I'm pregnant.'

The impact of her statement suffused Neil's face in vivid slow motion. He reached across the table and hugged her. His tie, which he hadn't bothered to remove since he got back from work, dipped into her lasagne.

'Mind your tie,' she said.

'Sod my tie,' said Neil, kissing her fiercely. There were tears in his eyes, which brought tears to her own. They sat back and regarded each other with delight, speechless. Someone behind Suzy was trying to get through to the bar. She hitched her chair in with an automatic apology. Whoever it was continued to bear down on her. She moved her chair out to one side, and turned to see a man in his fifties, obviously very drunk. His shoulders were narrow beneath a worn grey jacket and he needed a shave.

'Watch it, mate,' Neil cautioned lightly, still intent on Suzy. The man took another step into their table and put down his near-empty glass, misjudging the distance. He appeared to be collecting his balance so that he could spend it on a last trajectory to the bar. Neil pulled a face at Suzy, counselling her to ignore the man. But he ducked towards them, extending a finger. Suzy could see a rind of filth beneath the nail. She looked away, avoiding the man's phlegm-coloured gaze, and waited for him to speak. He said nothing, but continued to point. Drawing thick, deliberate breaths, glaring, he slowly swept his finger from Suzy to Neil, as though admonishing them. There was a moment when Suzy thought that Neil might do anything, even hit the man, but then the drunk took up his glass and lurched away to the bar.

'Charming,' remarked Neil, raising his own glass with relief. He squeezed her hand. She smiled at him, trying to erase the interruption and return to their joy. But it stayed with her. In bed that night, as Neil held his warm hand over her belly, murmuring the future, her pleasure was tainted with the memory of the drunk's gathered malevolence. She didn't speak about it. She held herself still and eventually Neil fell asleep. When she could hear that his breathing was uninterrupted and deep, she rolled away from beneath his hand and got up.

Downstairs, Suzy rifled her bag. At the bottom was the cheap brown envelope containing the chain letter, now crumpled, the ink of the address smeared by contact with a wet tissue. This time, she made herself read the whole page. It said that she would receive good luck within four days of receiving the letter, as long as she sent twenty copies of it out, also within four days. 'This is no joke,' she read. 'Send no money as fate has no price.' The letter listed those who had obeyed this instruction and had been rewarded with various sums of money, the most being three million dollars a South American woman had won in a lottery. It went on to state that someone called Gene Walsh had broken the chain and then lost his wife six days later. Another man called Delan Fairchild, it continued, threw the letter away and died within nine days. A third man had lost his job. The letter concluded with an account of an unnamed young woman in California who had ignored the instructions. 'She was plagued with various problems,' Suzy read, 'expensive car repairs. She finally typed the letter as promised and got a new car.' This concluding incident reassured Suzy. She had kept the letter for weeks longer than the stipulated ninety-six hours, but at least she hadn't thrown it away. The man in the pub had just been a warning.

Before she started work the next day, Suzy went to the newsagent and made twenty copies of the letter. She had to pay for twenty-one copies, because the first time she didn't position the sheet correctly on the machine, but after this they turned out crisply on the page. Then she went to the post office and bought stamps and envelopes.

Once she sat down at home to send the letters off, Suzy realised that twenty names were a lot to come up with. She didn't want to send the letters to her family, or her best friends. After some reflection, she sent one to Neil's boss, and to Mrs Reeves who she used to work for at the nursery. She still had the addresses of some parents from the nursery in her book, so she sent letters to them. But she was still far short of twenty. Suzy relented about her family and addressed a couple of envelopes to some cousins in Yorkshire she never saw. Then, disguising her writing by using capitals, she sent letters to all her cleaning clients. The remaining four addresses she took randomly from the phone book, pleased with her own belated initiative.

Even just posting the stack of envelopes made her feel less encumbered. She had a good morning cleaning for Mrs Walsh, a woman in her sixties whose husband earned a lot of money. They lived in a modern bungalow which was huge but very easy to keep clean. Mrs Walsh was a lively talker, and paid Suzy for the extra hour they always spent drinking coffee in the middle of her session. That day she asked Suzy if she needed a microwave, as they were getting a new model with a browning facility.

'There's nothing wrong with this one,' Mrs Walsh assured her. 'It works like a dream, really. But all my friends have got them so I thought I'd ask you.'

The microwave was unwieldy but not heavy, and Suzy managed to take it home with her on the bus. In return for the gift, Suzy had told Mrs Walsh about her pregnancy. She felt sure now that confirmation from the doctor was just a hoop to jump through. Mrs Walsh was thrilled for her. She had two grown-up children herself.

'It's the most wonderful thing in the world,' she assured Suzy. Thinking about it on the bus, cradling the microwave, Suzy could feel herself smiling. She felt light-headed with luck.

When she let herself into Eleanor and Greg's the next morning, her own chain letter was among the uncollected post scattered on the hall carpet. Suzy felt the guilt flooding her face as she tucked the letter between the other envelopes and made a neat pile to take through to the kitchen. Eleanor wasn't there. Suzy left the post on the table and went upstairs. From the landing, she could see that half of the bathroom was newly occupied by a large upended shape wrapped in layers of plastic sheeting.

'Scary, isn't it?' said Eleanor, making Suzy jump. She stood at her bedroom door, wearing a voluminous towelling dressing gown with a hood. 'It's the birthing pool. They delivered it at the weekend.'

'I thought you might already . . .' Suzy said. Eleanor grimaced. Her hair was crested at one side and she had clearly just woken up.

'I'm three days overdue,' she sighed, palming her eyes. 'D'you want a coffee?'

'I'll do it,' Suzy offered. 'You should be putting your feet up.' She was thinking of the letter waiting downstairs. Seeing Eleanor's small body so overwhelmed by pregnancy, it didn't seem fair. She could throw the envelope away before Eleanor even saw it and get another name out of the phone book instead. But Eleanor was already on her way downstairs.

'Don't worry,' she said. 'I'm trying to be as active as possible. If I haven't squeezed the little bugger out by Friday I'll be doing aerobics to bring it on.'

As they drank coffee together, Suzy tried to curb her gaze from veering to the post by Eleanor's elbow. Eleanor opened the envelope on the top of the pile, which looked as if it had come from her bank. But either their conversation or a desire for privacy detained her from making further progress. Once Suzy had drained her mug she had no choice but to leave the kitchen and get on with her work. By the time she had finished, Eleanor had moved into the living room to make phone calls. Suzy could hear her laughing as she went to replace the cleaning materials in their space beneath the kitchen sink. Her heart syncopating, Suzy riffled through the pile of opened post on the table. The chain letter had gone. She replaced the letters in exact position and moved to the large chrome pedal bin. She floored the pedal, hoisting the lid. The crumpled letter lay nested among ripped envelopes, already stained by a discarded teabag.

There was nothing she could do.

Fortunately, it was easy not to think about the letter once she had left Eleanor and Greg's. She had an appointment at the doctor's, and received official confirmation that she was pregnant, as she had known that she would. Afterwards Suzy went to the library and took out books about babies and what to do in pregnancy. She felt wonderful; not even tired, let alone sick. Neil was keen on her giving up work almost at once, but she told him that there was no point as long as she felt well and was able to get around. He couldn't argue: the extra money would be welcome for as long as she could earn it.

'All right,' he conceded, kissing the top of her head. 'But then we'll get *you* a cleaner.'

A week later, just as Suzy was about to leave the house for Eleanor and Greg's, the phone went. It was Greg. His voice sounded very young, although he was probably closer to forty than thirty. He was relieved to have caught her, he said.

'Ellie asked me to ring because she thinks something might be happening,' he explained nervously. 'You know, with the baby. So we wondered if you minded leaving it this week. We'll pay you, of course,' he added.

Suzy told him not to worry, and that she hoped everything went well. She was tantalised, but more than that, anxious. She could see the letter, so confidently discarded, sitting in the bin. The last thing they would think of would be to ring her when Eleanor had actually had the baby.

All through that day she sent them good thoughts. And when she let herself in the following week, there was Eleanor in the kitchen, breast-feeding a perfect bundle as Greg hovered over mother and child, soporific with pride. It was a girl, to be called Lydia. Her fierce, unsquashed little face was too new to resemble either of her parents. Everything had gone smoothly, Eleanor told her. Suzy stroked the cool, buttery skin of the baby's cheek, feeling as much relief as envy.

'Precious,' she breathed. She needn't have worried after all, she thought.

It was on the lunchtime news the next day. Suzy was stretched on the sofa, nursing her abdomen and talking to the tiny thing inside her. She had been sick for the first time that morning, which she found reassuring. It was a couple of seconds into the report before the image on the TV snagged at her attention. Then she sat up as though a hinge had snapped shut. Eleanor and Greg were slumped behind a long table flanked by grave-looking strangers, hedged in by microphones. Eleanor, hollow-eyed, mouthed tremulously. Suzy fumbled for the remote and switched off the mute button. 'Please, just give her back,' Eleanor was saying. 'You won't be in trouble, but she's ours, and we love her.' She started to sob, and Greg gathered her into his arms. A telephone number appeared at the bottom of the screen.

The newsreader delivered bald facts. Shortly after Suzy had left the previous afternoon, a woman had turned up at the house and introduced herself as the health visitor. Knowing that the health visitor was due to call at some point, Eleanor had let her in. Greg had gone out to the supermarket, and while Eleanor was in the kitchen making the woman a cup of tea, she had simply walked out of the house with the baby. Still weeping, but attempting to control herself, Eleanor gave a detailed description of the woman, who was in her mid-thirties. According to the police, it was likely that she had disguised herself with a wig and glasses. But they went on to say that they were confident they would find the baby sooner rather than later. The report ended on Eleanor and Greg's shocked, tear-bloated faces.

Suzy was sick again, heaving emptily. She didn't go out for her cleaning job. She stayed in front of the TV all afternoon, shocked, switching between news bulletins and Teletext to catch any developments. She rang up Neil at work, unable to stop herself breaking down as she told him what had happened. Her words dissolved into noisy sobbing. As the sobbing went on, Neil became bewildered by the force of her distress.

'They always find them, love,' he reassured her. 'The neighbours end up calling the police when they realise something dodgy's going on, a baby appearing from nowhere.'

Suzy was unconsoled. She knew what was happening, she wanted to tell him, and she knew why it had happened. But she hung up without saying anything more.

The evening news used the same footage of the press conference, joined by a computerised photofit of the woman who had taken the baby. She looked like nothing human, just hair and glasses. By morning, there was another brief statement from Greg, shot outside the house. 'We just hope whoever has Lydia is looking after her,' he said bleakly. This was shown on both the local and the national news. By the following day the story had dropped to a secondary item, and the day after that appeared only on the local bulletin, recycling the press conference images. Over the weekend, interest revived with the angle that Lydia's abductor might have taken her abroad; flight and ferry records were being checked and the cooperation of Interpol was being sought.

Through all this, Suzy barely slept or ate. Neil was so worried about her that at his insistence she cancelled all her clients. He urged her to think of their own baby. But she knew that their baby was safe, rooted inside her and growing. Their baby was safe because Eleanor and Greg's baby was gone. They were offering a reward for any information that might lead the police to their child. Neil mentioned this, hoping it would encourage her into optimism. Suzy remembered the phrase from the letter:

'Fate has no price,' she told him.

'What's that supposed to mean?' he asked. She turned herself away from him in the bed. When she shut her eyes she could see the discarded letter, the stain from the teabag like weak brown blood.

The next day, she let herself into Greg and Eleanor's house at her usual time. Greg called out from the kitchen, and rushed into the hall.

'Suzy,' he said, surprised.

She knew then that she shouldn't have come. Greg looked at her as though he had to concentrate to see her properly.

'We didn't think to ring,' he explained, rubbing his arms with non-existent cold. Eleanor was upstairs, he told her. She'd been given a sleeping pill. Even from a glimpse, Suzy could tell that the house was in chaos. A child's car seat decorated with pink and yellow teddies had tipped over against the hall table, its emptiness pushed to face the wall. Greg hovered, uncertain what to do.

'I could just sort things out down here if you like,' said Suzy softly.

Greg wetted his lips.

'It doesn't matter,' he said. 'Really. We'll pay you for the week.' Vaguely, he reached into the back pocket of his jeans. Suzy recoiled.

'No,' she said. 'Honestly.'

He smiled at her. 'We'll call you,' he said. 'When things are . . .' he mistrusted himself with the rest of the phrase. As they stood there, struggling for language, it came to Suzy what to do, as clearly as someone talking to her on the phone. Loud and clear. She felt herself smiling at him.

'It'll all be all right,' Suzy told him. 'I know there'll be news soon.' The words didn't seem to reach him. She tried again, touching his arm.

'Tell Eleanor I said so,' she urged. 'Tell her I said it'll all be all right.' But Greg didn't look like he would tell Eleanor. She would find out soon enough of course, but Suzy wished that she could have brought her some immediate comfort.

She could have taken a bus home but the walk calmed her. As soon as she got in she went straight to the phone book.

They didn't need a medical reason, she knew that. Termination, they called it. Like a terminus, where the buses stopped at the end of their route. And it was stopping with her, where she should have let it stop. With love all things are possible. Fate has no price.

Weather

Although she despised the mistrust implied by her own restraint, Teresa had waited for Ben to suggest they go away together. They had been going out for nearly six months, and he brought it up one night without Teresa even having to steer the conversation round, which was a relief. This was to be their first holiday as a couple, and most of the organisation devolved on Teresa, as Ben was going through a busy patch at work and she wasn't. Even though she had shown Ben the picture of the hotel in the brochure, and gone through the details with him more than once before booking, Teresa was nervous about taking responsibility for the choice. It was impossible to tell much, from a brochure. But Ben said he just wanted some peace and quiet, a rest. Teresa, less overworked than Ben, was looking forward to the good

weather. The travel agent had assured her that in Sicily in
May, it was reliably hot and sunny.

They arrived in Taormina at night to find that their hotel
was dingier and less imposing than its photo had suggested.
This was predictable, if disappointing. But their discontent
solidified as soon as they opened the door to their room. It
was at the end of a corridor and, being on a corner where
one wing of the building met another, oddly shaped.
Cramped at ground level, yet with a cavernously high ceiling, the room managed to offer both uncomfortable
confinement and an atmosphere of desolation. Ben marched
around, dodging items of brown furniture. Then, with his
hands on his hips, he glared out at the darkened view, which
was not, as it happened, the sea one they had requested.
Teresa felt knotted with responsibility. Personally, she was
prepared to give the room the benefit of the doubt.
Knowing the worst and accepting it was much better than
suffering in anticipation.

'Nope,' said Ben, flatly furious. He turned and stalked out
to complain to the manager, slamming the door as he went.
Since she had been going out with Ben, Teresa had done anything she could to prevent herself from seeing him this
angry. Agitated, she only wished she had persuaded him to
overcome his reservations about the food in Crete. After ten
minutes Ben returned, unmollified. Nothing could be done
until the day manager was on duty. The two of them spent
an irritable night, not touching. The bed at least was comfortable.

The next morning the sun seared a sky of deep, expansive
blue. Even with the less desirable view, Mount Etna was

visible, crisply defined and unlikely in the distance. Ben
became more cheerful and affectionate. After a conversation
with the day manager they were moved to a better room,
conventionally shaped, which looked out on to the sea. And
when they went out to find the pool, the hotel almost
entirely redeemed itself. The pool was reached by a winding
path of volcanic rock, bounded by magenta arcs of
bougainvillaea. Tiny lizards skittered out of sight as they
passed and, at each bend, the sea and coast revealed themselves in different, stunning proportions. The pool itself
was on a terrace, ringed by cypresses, its water like an
abstracted portion of the glittering sea behind it. Beside it
were white loungers, some protected by umbrellas, and a
well-maintained bar with a canopy, where a young man
around their age wiped glasses and listened to Italian pop on
the radio.

'This is really nice, isn't it?' said Ben, leading the way to
a lounger. The weight of Teresa's anxiety was displaced as
suddenly as if she had dived into the pool.

It turned out that there was a supplementary charge for
the umbrellas – not that they minded. They spent most of
the next few days at the pool, reading thick novels, swimming, dozing, drinking the small bottles of Fanta served at
the bar and chatting in disconnected sentences. They staggered in for lunch, which was part of their half-board at the
hotel, and depending on how full they felt, either returned
to the pool or took a siesta in their room. They usually had
sex at some point during the siesta. At night, they enjoyed
getting changed into semi-smart clothes, applying after-
shave and perfume respectively, and finding a bar to have a

drink in before they settled on a place for dinner. Then they walked off a little of their drunkenness and satiety, hoping to blend in with the smartly dressed Italians out on *passeggiata*, perhaps stopping for an ice-cream or another drink, and returned to the hotel. They had more sex, and slept soundly.

After three days, Ben's skin was freckled and red, and he made jokes more frequently than he did in England. Teresa had turned a honeyed brown, and she laughed in genuine appreciation of Ben's jokes. Over their swordfish or *pasta alla norma*, they wistfully discussed the viability of selling their flats, moving to Italy and working through e-mail and ISDN. But when Ben started to talk quite earnestly one night about handing in his notice, Teresa nervously pointed out that in practical terms, living in Italy would be impossible. She'd heard that you had to wait up to six months just to have a phone line installed. Ben accepted this, a little grudgingly. He played with a piece of tomato left on his plate.

'I really, really hate work, you know,' he told her. She was surprised by his intensity.

'Well, if you really feel like that you should leave,' she said.

'What else would I do?' He cut the tomato in two with the flat of his fork.

'I don't know. You could do a course,' she suggested.

'What on?'

'I don't know.'

She picked up the piece of tomato from his plate and ate it.

'I think I'm going to leave anyway,' he said. She couldn't tell if he meant it or not. The thought of him leaving work stirred a current of panic in her stomach. Ben was stable. It was one of the qualities she most appreciated in him.

After the fourth day of the holiday, the turn of the holiday as Teresa thought of it, because there were less days remaining than days they had already spent, the weather broke. They woke to find the view of Etna erased by heavy banks of cloud. Ben groaned as he stuck his head and torso out of the window, testing the temperature in the blank grey air. Without the sun, it was at least ten degrees cooler. He threw himself hopelessly back on to the bed, and became absorbed in peeling burnt patches of skin from his shoulders. Teresa recognised the need for initiative.

'What do you want to do?' she asked.

Ben shrugged. Teresa, feeling tender toward him, leafed through their guidebook and suggested a trip to Syracuse.

'What's there?' he asked. She read out excerpts from the guide, promising points of interest in the old part of the city and detailing the size of the Greek amphitheatre. 'The second largest outside Greece,' she mentioned, encouragingly. There was also a cave, called the Ear of Dionysius, with amazing acoustics.

'You know what I'm like about acoustics,' said Ben. Teresa knew that his sarcasm meant he'd resigned himself to her suggestion.

After breakfast, they took the crowded, cleanly efficient train, reaching Syracuse in just over an hour. Even here, further down the coast, the low cloud still closed around them. Ben grumbled about this as the train pulled in.

'I thought the travel agent said the weather was always good.'

'She did. It probably won't last,' Teresa assured him, with no conviction whatsoever. She was beginning to feel slightly panicked. Ben had barely spoken on the train, and his irritability seemed to exceed any reasonable response to the weather. During the walk from the station to the old town, she chattered about a previous trip she had made to Italy with an old boyfriend. She told at least three funny stories, of which she was the butt, while making it clear that the old boyfriend was a dud in comparison with Ben. But his restlessness didn't lift. Deciding that her vivacity was probably what was getting on his nerves, Teresa then determined to be silent. Even when they passed some Roman foundations mentioned in the guidebook, she chose to let them go by without comment.

The old town turned out to be a clustered warren of dilapidated buildings with TVs gabbling invisibly from within. Lank pieces of clothing hung from windows, or occasionally, on lines strung between dwellings. The narrow streets were shadowed by the tenements, and Ben and Teresa had to pick their way along the damp, uneven paving. This was scattered with rubbish and sporadically smelt of piss.

'Charming,' Ben observed, as they passed a bony cat burrowing into the reeking contents of a burst bin liner. 'It must get better than this.'

Teresa said she was sure it would, and indeed, after ten minutes or so, they came to a piazza facing the sea on one side, with an ancient but functioning fountain and a reassuring smattering of tourists. Teresa located the fountain in her guidebook, and read out the excerpt to Ben.

'Are those authentic Roman fag packets, then?' asked Ben. He pointed to an outlet for the water, where a bolus of leaves and sodden Marlboro packets strained to escape against a metal grille.

'You always have to do that,' Teresa heard herself saying.

'What?' For the first time that day, Ben was giving her his full attention.

'Nothing.' She closed the guidebook and put it back in the bag. 'You feeling hungry yet?'

'Yeah. What d'you mean, I always have to do that?'

'Nothing.' She looked around, lighting on a café with a few plastic chairs and tables placed outside. 'That place looks OK.'

They ate mediocre pizzas, largely in silence. Ben left more of his than Teresa did hers. The pizzas were no worse than the ones they'd had in Taormina, but the surroundings, and of course the weather, made them seem less appetising. Seeing the crusts that littered Ben's plate, the detritus of judgement, Teresa felt a surge of hatred towards him. She compensated for this by lifting his hand, which was on the table, and kissing it.

'It's good being on holiday, isn't it?' she said.

He didn't respond.

After a brief but exasperating round of 'What d'you want to do?' 'I don't mind', they took a bus out to the amphitheatre, which was on the outskirts of the town. There was a park at the entrance, which they agreed to leave until later. Following signs, they crossed scrubby grassland dotted with other tourists, and reached the huge bowl of the theatre. Its bleached structure, almost intact, pushed through the earth like a gigantic set of broken teeth. Normally, Teresa and Ben might have tested the acoustics, with one of them standing on the stage and the other up in the audience, but neither of them suggested this. Teresa took a few photographs, circumspectly. Ben sat on one of the stone terraces and smoked. He frowned when Teresa pointed the camera at him, so she took a picture of the stage instead. A tour group swarmed above them, then moved away, towards the park. The American tour guide's voice carried, emphatically conveying dates.

'Do you want to see the rest, or get something to drink, or do something else . . .' Teresa asked Ben, lightly. He shrugged.

'Shall we see the park, then?'

'If you like,' he said. His tone was utterly flat. By now Teresa felt as though she was brimming with some dangerously corrosive liquid, which might spill out of her mouth if she allowed herself to speak. She concentrated on looking at the flowers which flanked the path. They were exotic and various. The only ones she knew by name were the geometric spikes of acanthus flowers. She refrained from comment.

After a couple of minutes, signs informed them that they had reached the Ear of Dionysius.

'May as well go in,' Teresa suggested. Ben grimaced assent.

From outside, the Ear appeared as a vast fissure in a steep escarpment of rock. The fissure widened slightly at ground

level, forming an entrance shaped like an elongated triangle.
Teresa led the way. The cave, lit only by the daylight that fil-
tered through the narrow entrance, immediately opened
into a vast, vaulted space. Ben and Teresa looked at each
other, meeting in the surprise of this. Then they broke away
and moved around separately in the cool, belittling silence.
There was a floor of soft sand, and undulating, pocked walls
formed by the rock. Tentatively, Teresa tilted back her head
and pushed air through her pursed lips. The polite 'wooooo'
that she made ascended far in blackness to the cave's invisible roof. Just as it seemed lost it returned, amplified into a
ghostly chord.

Ben smiled. 'Cool.' He tipped his head back and said
'hello', authoritatively. It rang down on them, not echoed,
but formed into a sound both larger and purified. He tried
again. 'Hello hello hello?' came back as a mournful, enquir-
ing triplet. Teresa watched him. He had his arms folded. It
made him look critical.

'If you can just make your way . . .' Ben pulled a face.
The American tour guide was ushering his group through
the narrow arch. The women were dressed in floral smocks
and the men in shorts, all in pristine gym socks and sandals,
like a Sunday school outing accelerated to old age. Their
exclamations as they entered the cave created an eddying
swell of noise until the guide asked for their attention.
Trained to obedience, the group mutely gathered round
him. The guide was about twenty years younger than his
charges, with elaborate syntax and a beard. Ben pulled
another face at Teresa, meaning that he wanted to leave.
Teresa pretended not to have seen him. She peered up

sightlessly into the dark. To be so far from home, in a hole in the earth, moved her.

'. . . and the Emperor's prisoners, reputedly incarcerated in here, are said to have eased their burden by singing . . .' The guide's voice was blithely invasive.

'Treese——' Ben hissed at her, nodding to the entrance, already moving towards it. Teresa motioned impatiently to him, turned back. More than anything, she wished that she was on her own. This thought, once released, seemed to come back to her like the noises in the cave, resonant.

The bearded guide gave Teresa a small professional smile as she passed. He was waving his arms expansively, counting his group in. Out of the silence, the old men and women started to sing 'Frère Jacques'. Immediately, the parts of the tune swelled and filled the cave with overlapping crests of melody, reproducing into a thousand voices. Despite himself, Ben stopped to listen. Wave after wave of sound broke over them, its entirety building until it extinguished the possibility of other senses and emotions. It was the song of angels, consuming and perfect. It might have gone on for ever. Finally, it stopped. Silence hung for a second or two as the members of the tour group beamed at each other, shy with the beauty they'd created.

Outside, Ben took Teresa's hand for the first time that day. 'Sorry,' he said, squeezing it.

By the early evening, as they were taking the train back to Taormina, the sun was visible, and all the edges to the mountains. The cloud had drifted out to sea. The weather report on the television in their hotel room displayed a big red sun slapped on the coastline. Commanded by Ben,

Teresa came out of the bathroom from brushing her teeth to see it.

'It'll be hotter than ever tomorrow,' he said; then: 'You look nice.' He pulled Teresa down on the bed beside him, and pushed her hair back from her face.

'What's wrong?' he asked.

'Toothpaste,' she told him. She went back into the bathroom and spat.

'You know,' he called after her, 'I've almost definitely decided to hand in my notice.'

Teresa turned off the tap, deliberating. From the door she said, 'You were a bit – it was a bit difficult today.'

Ben pointed the remote at the TV, turning it off. He held out his hand for her. He had a soft smile on his face, and looked very young.

'It was just the weather,' he said. 'It's going to be great tomorrow.'

She put the toothbrush in its glass, bristles facing away from his. 'What if it isn't?'

Ben jerked his hand, emphasising its offer of contact. Although disinclined, Teresa walked over to him.

'It'll blow over,' he said, confidently. 'It always does.'

Open Wide

Sally was at her grandfather's funeral. The day was grey but warm, and during an exceptionally sodden June the fact that the rain held off for the whole enterprise seemed miraculous. Guests consoled themselves with this, yet Sally felt that the occasion demanded a driving rain, as in films, which was the closest she had been to a funeral before that day. She regretted that the weather hadn't complied with her sense of what was appropriate; it might have rendered the whole occasion more real. Her grandfather had been a keen amateur actor, and perhaps persuaded by the thespian associations of the velvet curtains in the chapel of rest, he had opted for cremation. Deprived of a full graveside scene, it was difficult for Sally to imagine that the coffin's decorous exit through the curtains in any way precluded the trip backstage her grandad had always expected after a performance.

Back at her brother's house, Sally stood eating fruit cake with a cluster of small and vivacious Welsh relatives she hadn't seen since she was a little girl. She'd had a lot to drink, and was not alone in this state. As Sally made animated conversation on a range of subjects she cared nothing about, producing opinions where she had never previously entertained thoughts (on Michael Barrymore, traffic speed cameras, organic food) something hard cropped up in a bite of cake. Seeing a glint of silver, she thought fleetingly that she'd got a lucky charm or a silver coin in her portion, as with Christmas pudding. But dislodging a sultana from the morsel on her plate, she saw that the silver in fact belonged to a filling. What she was looking at was a sizeable part of a tooth, partly filled.

'I've got a tooth in my cake,' she exclaimed to the Welsh relatives, who recoiled from their own portions in sudden alarm. Then, probing her mouth with her tongue, 'It's mine,' she announced. Expecting a jolt of pain to follow this discovery, Sally was grateful for the alcohol padding out her edges. A tentative reconnaissance with her tongue established no more than a tenderness and a crater around a left lower molar. She put the bit of tooth in her handbag, neatly wrapped in a paper napkin decorated with intertwined silver horseshoes and bells. The napkins were left over from her brother's wedding.

When she rang Jamie that night, Sally turned the tooth into her major funeral anecdote. There was no issue surrounding the fact that he hadn't accompanied her that day.

Jamie had never met her grandfather, and they were both agreed that having sex regularly didn't equate to an automatic escort service.

'It'd be funnier if it was someone else's tooth you found,' Jamie pointed out.

'But horrible,' she objected. 'Not as bad as a fingernail, though. I think I'd've been sick if I'd found a fingernail. Even my own.'

The next day, Sally made an appointment with her dentist. The dentist was listed under D, for dentist, in her address book, and she could not remember his name when the receptionist asked her who she usually saw. Her visits were far from habitual. She never abided by the rule of the six-monthly check-up and it was over two years since she had been, at that time also to replace a lost filling. She was ashamed of this laxity, and every time she visited she resolved to look after her teeth more systematically, but somehow never got round to it.

The plain fact was that the dentist terrified her.

Sally sternly dismissed the stab of panic in her gut when she woke on the morning of her dental appointment. She was close to the delivery date for her Ph.D. thesis and she had plenty of work to do. The thesis – 'Notions of Hospitality in Roman Life 85–22 BC' – was essentially complete, and the only real work that remained was the footnotes and bibliography. Sally relished the escape these chores presented from finicking thought. They were work, but they made none of the anxious demands that she associated with work. She relegated the dentist to the margins of her concentration as she checked the references for some

erotic floor tiles discovered near Vicenza. Then, forty minutes before her appointment, Sally switched off her laptop
and brushed and flossed her teeth with determined thor-
oughness and serenity.

Even during the short bus journey she managed largely to
displace her anxiety with concern over an unattributed quo-
tation. But as soon as she walked into the waiting room
Sally felt the full, visceral force of her dread. The warm
stench of antiseptic and the deranged wasp whine of drills
invoked a nostalgic wave of terror. She gave her name and
sat. It was only at the dentist's and while on planes that she
truly appreciated the frail constraint of her own civilised
behaviour. Acting on her instincts, she would be exploiting
the adrenalin coursing through her system to sprint out of
the surgery and down the muggy high street. This instinct
burgeoned with each dead minute spent in the waiting
room. Sally took a couple of exhausted magazines from the
pile in front of her. She was turning the front page of the
second one when the receptionist called her name and
instructed her to go to surgery three.

'Sally? Hi.'

Sally wasn't sure that she remembered the dentist from
her last visit. He was young, with a smile that flashed an
exemplary band of white incisors. Or maybe you just
noticed dentists' teeth more. They were not like hair-
dressers, she reflected, who flaunted lanker and more
dishevelled heads of hair the more skilled and expensive
they became. The teeth had to inspire confidence.

'Come in,' the dentist commanded, as Sally hovered at
the door. He gestured to the empty chair. Sally tried not to

take in the array of hostile delving, boring and gouging implements that crowded every peripheral surface. She sat in the chair, which was upright. The dental nurse kept her back to Sally, fiddling intently with things that rattled on steel trays.

'Now what are we going to be doing today?' the dentist asked. His thick brown hair had a healthy sheen, like a child's.

Sally rattled off a nervy précis of the fruit cake incident, finishing with a declaration that she was 'a nervous patient'.

'OK, let's just take a look, then,' said the dentist.

He tipped the examination chair to horizontal and swung round on his castored chair in one frictionless flourish. The nurse fixed a blue plastic bib around Sally's neck. Sally closed her eyes, tightly. The dental mirror introduced itself between her cheek and gum, an instrument probed, pain shot up into her head and she uttered an involuntary bovine murmur of protest.

'Sorry about that. Certainly a bit of a problem there,' the dentist intoned unapologetically. 'I'm just going to have a general look round now.' The mirror and probe tapped around her mouth, accompanied by the dentist's incomprehensible verbal semaphore to the nurse. Sally's mouth felt expanded to Grand Canyon proportions. A Grand Canyon shot through with nerves eagerly transmitting pain signals to her neural centres. She reflected that if they were working to scale the mirror would be the size of a satellite dish and the probe about as large as . . . Nelson's column? She jumped as the probe prodded near the gum.

'M.O.,' the dentist repeated to his assistant. Occasionally

he said 'OK'. Finally he told Sally that she could close her mouth, then tipped her chair upright and wheeled himself away to a Formica-topped counter. He scribbled on her card for a couple of seconds. His assistant, who looked too young and sulky to be working, lolled her mobile pelvis against her bit of counter. Sally sat with her hands folded in her lap.

'We're just going to take some X-rays because it has been a while since your last visit—'

'Sorry—' she interjected.

'Then we'll have a little chat.'

Sally cooperated by holding uncomfortable bits of plastic in her mouth while the assistant disappeared to press the exterior X-ray button. In front of her was a sign which read 'Please let us know if you are pregnant.' She wondered if she could be. Jamie would have a lot to say about it if she was. The assistant led her back into the surgery, where the dentist sat with his ballpoint poised above Sally's chart.

'That's lovely,' he said. 'We'll take care of the broken molar today, and then you'll need a couple of appointments. As you say, it's been a while and there is quite a bit of work to do.'

'How much?' asked Sally.

'There's quite a few fillings.'

'Oh. How many?'

'Ten.'

Sally pointed out that she hadn't that many teeth left unfilled, but the dentist countered with the fact that the bits of tooth notionally surrounding the existing fillings were on the point of disintegration. Then he summoned the needle and tipped her to horizontal again.

The brutally large needle, inadvertently glimpsed before she clenched her eyes shut, seared a deep line of pain into her gum that traced far up into her skull. The pain lasted slightly longer than she thought she could bear, then was over. The dentist retracted the hypodermic and said they would wait a couple of minutes. He left her outside the surgery to decide her method of payment as she waited to turn numb. When the sulky assistant called her in, Sally anxiously palpated her lip.

'Does it feel numb?' asked the dentist.

'Not very,' said Sally doubtfully.

The dentist reassured her that if there was any pain, he would stop and wait until the numbness had spread. The drill started, Sally contracted, gripping the arms of the chair, and he went in. A couple of seconds passed, and then she located an area on her mammoth toothscape, not of pain, exactly, but of incipient pain, a retarded message that pain might well be in the offing if the drilling continued there. She ululated a mild warning. The dentist said OK, and continued to drill. Each time he strayed into the dangerous area, Sally made the same noise. Then, at the bit's passing stroke, the message arrived. A different pain than the one from the probe or the needle. Those had been hot, thin wires; this was a massive organ chord of pain that resonated even after the dentist had removed the drill.

'Hurts,' she gagged indistinctly, but feelingly.

'Sorry,' said the dentist. He went in again. Sally felt her neck cramping from the tension in her muscles. She concentrated on letting her body release a fraction of its rigidity. It wasn't easy. At any moment the drill's blind edge might catch that vulnerable point. Sure enough, within seconds it found the site of pain, and this time her cry expressed her outrage. The dentist stopped drilling.

'There will be a bit of discomfort even with the Novocaine,' he said, almost reproachfully. Sally found the euphemism appalling. Discomfort was pins and needles, or a shoe that rubbed, not this agony thrilling every nerve ending in her body.

'Hurts,' she reiterated adamantly. It sounded like 'harhhhs'.

'I know,' the dentist soothed her. 'We'll just numb you up a bit more.'

She felt a liquid lapping over the afflicted site, then tasted bitterness as it flowed on to her tongue. Her throat contracted automatically, but the suction hose snatched her saliva away.

'That should be OK now,' said the dentist. Sally tried to believe him, but as soon as the drill started again she was flinching against the expectation of pain. He drilled now in staccato bursts, barely making contact before he had whisked the point away. Very slightly, she began to relax, becoming accustomed to the butterfly kiss rhythm of the pain he inflicted. There was only this, the noise and the tides of pain, each wave dying down as the next reached its crest. Finally, unimaginably, he shut the drill down.

'OK, have a good rinse out,' he commanded. Sally opened her eyes and sat upright. She swilled lurid pink liquid from the plastic cup at her side then ineffectually drooled it, spangled with motes of filling and tooth, into the midget basin.

The dentist lifted his hands, translucently gloved, in a beatific attitude. 'I've finished the first half of your root canal,' he informed her, with self-conscious drama.

Sally was taken aback. She hadn't known that she was going to have a root canal. Before her unresponsive palate could frame any objection she was swung back into the chair and had her injured gum packed with some malleable substance that the dentist assured her would harden to form a temporary covering. She would have to have a crown put on the tooth, he said, and produced a dummy set of hinged teeth set in overly pink gums as an aid to explanation. He removed the display crown and replaced it as he spoke, to show her the desirable snugness of the fit. There was, of course, no mention made of pain. Sally told the dentist that she couldn't afford to have the private, more durable crown. She would have to settle for the unreliable subsidised kind. He accepted this with smiling blandness.

As Sally walked out of the surgery and down the street to catch her bus, an invisible force dealt a chopping blow to her shins. Shaken, she saw that she had failed to notice a glass-topped coffee table that formed part of a sprawling pavement display of junk shop stock. The junk shop owner balefully admonished her to watch where she was going. She apologised, feeling dazed, as though she'd wandered on to the street from the scene of a traffic accident.

By the time she got home the extra Novocaine the dentist had administered had found its full force. Half her face was no longer working. In a bid for decisive action Sally switched the kettle on, then remembered the dentist's adjuration about no hot drinks for at least three hours. She switched the kettle off and rang Jamie instead. He was slightly cagey when she invited him round, since they had made no prior arrangement.

'It's not your grandad, is it?' he asked warily.

'No, it's my teeth,' she mumbled.

Jamie hadn't a single filling. In keeping with his general bodily integrity, his poreless skin and 20/20 vision and washboard stomach, his straight teeth were covered with peerless white enamel. They withstood his infantile crunching of sweeties as his musculature was impervious to its lack of exercise, and his liver to drinking. Sally was only half joking when she called him her *Übermensch*.

They started to make love as soon as Jamie was through the door. Sally grabbed at him when he entered as though sheer horniness had led her to call him at an unusual time. She avoided kissing him with her desensitised, tender mouth. It made her brutal and inventive.

'Get on the bed,' she said, thickly.

Jamie, surprised and stirred, complied. She pushed him back, and started to undo his belt. The sex they usually had was urgent, but tended to decorum. They both preferred to keep the lights on, however. This time, Sally snapped the lamp off. She had no desire to see Jamie's face. Or rather, she desired quite strongly not to see it.

She pulled Jamie's belt from its loops and started on his flies, which were buttoned. Jamie reared up appreciatively. She used a tap of the belt buckle to keep him in place. He subsided, with a yelp of surprise. It had pleasure at the end of it. He caught hold of the belt buckle, which was heavy brass, and pulled Sally to him. They struggled for a few seconds, then Jamie's strength told and he pinned Sally to the bed. She rolled her mouth away from his kisses.

'Hurt me,' she commanded.

Jamie's face betrayed astonishment, although sexual etiquette prevented him giving it voice. Sally slapped at his face, light, provocative taps. 'Go on.' She tapped harder. 'Go on.' He caught her hands, irritated. She pulled, so that he had to force his grip. Then she nipped the flesh of his shoulder with her canines. It was difficult to judge the force of her bite, given the numbness of her mouth. He bucked away, howling. For a second, Sally thought that she had harmed the moment, and that Jamie would get off the bed and leave. But then he turned back and slammed her flat on the bed. And he hurt her.

'You're drooling,' Jamie said afterwards, slightly disgusted.

Sally touched the dead side of her lip. It was wet. She went to look at herself in the bathroom mirror and wiped the saliva from her chin. She couldn't feel it. Her skin was bleached of any colour and the left side of her face was softened and impassive. She was reminded of her grandad the last time she has seen him in the hospital, after his stroke. Fatigue overwhelmed her. She went back to the bedroom and lay on the bed next to Jamie, foetally curled. The horseshoe weal of her own teeth was branded on his otherwise blank shoulder.

When she woke it was dark and cold and her mouth was enormous with pain. Jamie had gone. She looked for a note but he hadn't left one, which wasn't unusual. Sally winkled out four ancient paracetamol from the debris in a neglected drawer. She couldn't bear to put the light on. She took the pills with a glass of water and, as she waited for the disinformation they carried to reach her brain, the tears sprang up from her throat. She didn't know how long she wept through the damage. On and on it went, on and on, until at last the pain began to seem normal.

Credit in Lieu

Janet Sleaford spent quite a lot of her time in London, returning items to department stores. Since the death of her husband eight years before, she had made ever more frequent journeys up from her home in Gloucestershire, with shopping as her principal object and recreation. The trouble was that Janet's taste required a long exposure, and it was not until days after a trip that the shape of her feelings towards a lamp or a blouse achieved satisfactory definition, more often than not revealing them as utter disasters. So once again she would catch a morning train to Paddington, optimistic about rectifying her mistakes.

Janet knew that this flawed cycle of consumption irritated her daughter Tina, who lived in London, but then much about her did. And although Tina wasn't aware of it, she made a substantial contribution to Janet's retail gaffes, since it was so often the sight of her, standing with her weight on one hip and glowering, that caused Janet to lose the thread of the labyrinthine internal argument which was leading her in one direction or the other, and panicking, plump blankly for an object in close proximity. Clothes were even worse. Janet never tried them on, which drove Tina mad.

'For God's sake, I don't mind waiting, Mother!'

She would urge Janet to the brink of the overheated and undersegregated changing rooms, but on this matter Janet always remained obdurate. In fact, to spare Tina's wrath, Janet only exchanged a portion of the clothes which she bought and would never wear. Despite this, Tina had her suspicions.

'What happened to that green blouse, the one with the funny collar?'

'Oh I wear it all the time, darling.'

There was no way for Tina to verify her mother's claims, since she saw Janet only on her days in London. And latterly, Janet had taken to visiting during the week, when Tina was at work. On these occasions she shopped alone and met her daughter for lunch, when she could dwell purely on the triumphant aspects of her morning, the reductions discovered and bargains achieved.

When Janet started this bifurcation of pleasure and responsibility, she felt so guilty that she brought Tina a present, an Italian coffeemaker from John Lewis with various obscure attachments. Tina expressed gratitude, although not without adding that she and her boyfriend, Julian, had largely given up drinking coffee. The next time, Janet brought her a light which clipped to the book you were reading in bed, so that you didn't disturb the person sleeping next to you. It had taken her fancy as she was returning a desk set at Debenhams. Tina remarked that Julian was the one who suffered from insomnia.

'You shouldn't waste your money on me,' she added, with a stern emphasis on waste. Tina wasted nothing, temporal or material. She worked, very efficiently, as a fundraiser for a musical charity. She rarely shopped, and when she did it was the culmination of a considered need. Tina had never in her life bought anything impulsively, and she only ever had cause to return an item if it proved faulty (although this was seldom, since Tina read *Which?* and restricted herself to brands acclaimed for their reliability). Janet wondered at this. In truth, the only time she didn't enjoy shopping was when she actually needed something. Then choice transformed itself from something glamorous, the consideration of myriad possible lives, into something oppressive, an equation with one right answer and any number of potential errors. It produced in her much the same feeling as many of her conversations with Tina.

Janet didn't allow herself to dwell on this association, which chafed her like something ill-fitting. She preferred to concentrate on the positive. After all, their new routine seemed to suit Tina, since she took her to nice places for lunch and seemed comparatively relaxed. And by the fourth such meeting, Janet thought nothing of coming to the table without a gift. Still, she was not so easy about their relations that upon buying a new winter coat – naturally without trying it on – she relished sharing this information with her daughter. Arriving at the restaurant, Janet gratefully accepted the waitress's offer to spirit her bags away. This deprived Tina's curiosity of any material target. Janet then glossed over the fruits of her shopping spree, and instead encouraged Tina to talk about her difficulties in selling her flat in Ealing. Although Tina was animated, Janet's attention was distracted by thoughts of her coat.

The coat had been a large investment, almost five hundred pounds, and Janet's doubts were already beginning to amass on the tube back to Paddington. These doubts became ponderous the following day, after a lengthy session in front of her wardrobe mirror, and critical the day after that, when she met a friend of hers who was wearing an unflattering garment in a similar shade of deepest purple.

It puts years on her, thought Janet in alarm, and steeled herself to make the trip to London. She was too ashamed to ring up Tina and tell her she would be in town so soon after her last visit. This would be strictly a guerrilla operation, she decided. Get in, return the coat and, God willing, find a suitable alternative. She was even prepared to try things on, and to that end took extreme care that morning in applying make-up, to buffer the assault of the mirrors. There was also the prospect of Christmas shopping, it being well into November, but this, Janet admonished herself, was to be an ancillary pursuit. Fortunately, she didn't have that many Christmas presents to worry about any more. Since her husband's death, the dutiful tithe of minor relatives and absent friends had dwindled considerably.

Selfridges loomed out of the scorched autumn air, hieratic and reassuring. Of all the department stores, it was

Janet's favourite. Although she divided her time fairly between them all, as with children, it was difficult to deny the pull she felt to this section of Oxford Street. They suited each other. Soon, she knew, she would be relieved of the burden of her bad choice.

She entered by way of the food hall and made for the coffee shop. On the way she paused to buy an imported packet of Florentines, possibly as part of a Christmas gift for the cleaner she referred to as her daily woman, although she came to Janet's house twice a week. Janet was quite fond of Florentines herself, when not abstaining in habitual deference to her figure. Just as well to have them, either way, she thought. She loosened the scarf she was wearing at her throat. It was warm in the store and she wished that she had worn something less encumbering than her bouclé suit.

Upstairs in Ladies' Outerwear, they were charming about the return of the coat. Janet had a passing familiarity with some of the assistants, but the girl who processed her return and filled out the resulting credit slip was new to her. She had a pretty, quizzical face, and reminded Janet slightly of Tina, although Tina was some years older. Janet told her that she was going to look around for another coat.

'Just say if you need anything,' said the girl.

Janet worked her way systematically through the rails, picking out anything that seemed vaguely suitable and trying it on. She didn't have much luck. She was a small, large-breasted woman and every garment she tried engulfed her, hiding her still dainty waist and making her look ungainly and squat. Examining herself in the mirror, Janet tried to stave off a prickly feeling of incipient nausea. Her image was drained and elderly, although perhaps the lights, or the unyielding black of the coat she was trying, were responsible for this. The assistant's fresh face darted into the reflection as a cruel contrast, scotching at least her theory about the lights.

'Not really you, is it?' she said kindly. 'I think . . .' She held up another coat, 'a *warmer* colour.'

The coat was the colour of a conker, and it seemed, as far as Janet could ever tell with these things, to suit her. It was very plain, and unvoluminously cut, and Janet wondered if anything so discreet could possibly be worth nearly five hundred pounds. But she could bear to look at herself in it, and the assistant was enthusiastic.

'It was made for you, really,' she said. Janet was practically decided. She took one more look in the mirror, and as she did, everything around her yawed and then contracted, sounds receded as though a volume control had been sharply switched down, and the visible world funnelled away into the distance. Oh no, was all Janet thought. This *oh no* reverberated in her skull until it too dissolved into darkness. An unfathomable time passed.

The next things Janet saw were white squares, punctuated by black dots. These were the ceiling boards. She was lying on the floor of Ladies' Outerwear, with her head cradled in the lap of the pretty assistant.

'Are you OK?' the girl asked.

'How stupid,' said Janet, trying to sit up.

'Best stay there,' the assistant urged, restraining her at the shoulders. Her boss trotted over, tight-mouthed and clumsy with panic, carrying a plastic cup of water. She gave it to the assistant, who held it out for Janet.

'We're calling an ambulance,' the manager told the girl, afraid, it seemed, to address Janet in any way directly.

'Oh please don't,' Janet heard herself say. 'Really, it's nothing serious.'

'She should go to the hospital,' the manager told the assistant. 'Just to be checked out. It could be her heart.'

'It was just a dizzy spell,' said Janet, beginning to dislike her. 'I would be grateful if you could call me a taxi. I'll go to my daughter's.'

They complied, and she was accompanied out to a cab. The chill between door and door sliced away the last soft edges of her dizziness. Janet gave the driver the name of Tina's road and settled back into the seat. The traffic, nearing lunchtime, was beginning to clot, and they progressed with only an occasional, opportunistic burst of speed.

Janet realised that Tina wouldn't be at home, but she felt calm about this. She would go to the estate agents handling the sale of her daughter's flat and explain to them who she was. They would have a spare set of keys. Once they'd let her in, she would wait for Tina to return. She didn't want to disturb her at work, and she preferred not to mention her loss of consciousness, suspecting that Tina would view it as a lapse for which only her mother could be held responsible.

The trip to Ealing took nearly an hour, although the driver couldn't be blamed. Janet got out at the estate agents' office. Tina's flat was one of the photos in the window. The manager was out at lunch, so Janet explained her problem to his assistant, a youth with livid little ranges of acne around his discouragingly slack mouth.

'We can't let you in unless you've made an appointment to view the property,' he maintained.

'But I'm Miss Sleaford's mother,' she objected.

'Sorry', he told her, 'it's procedure. We've got no way of verifying you are her mother, as such, so obviously we couldn't leave you in the property on your own, as I say. Sorry.'

He wouldn't be moved, even when she lost her temper. Janet gave up and went outside to ring Tina, since the assistant wouldn't permit her to use his phone. At Tina's office, an impersonal voice told her that Tina was out for the day. Janet was beginning to feel despondent, until it occurred to her that this might mean Tina was at home after all, off sick. Heartened by the possibility, she walked the few streets from the estate agents to Tina's flat. A few grudging flakes of snow were emerging from the white sky. It would be all right, thought Janet, it was always all right once you were inside, and warm, and all the nicer for having been deprived of it. But Tina's flat was unresponsive to her knocking and ringing, clearly empty. One of those days. The best thing to do was to cut her losses and go home. At least, she consoled herself, she was feeling herself again.

Before she left, Janet bent to pick up a cairn of sweet wrappers and dead leaves that the wind had driven into one corner of Tina's doorway. It was no impression to make on people, coming round to view the place.

Seeing no cabs in the empty streets, Janet walked to a phone box and called one. She had a card in her purse, for a cab company, and asked them for the price to Paddington so that they couldn't cheat her. She felt rather proud of herself for being so resourceful. Many of her friends made a fuss about coming to London, women she knew said they hadn't been into town for years, they'd be scared to now, but she was undaunted, even when something like this happened, which clearly was far from ideal. And she did have her coat, Janet reminded herself, opening the bag to catch a glimpse of its warm brown. She waited by the phone box for the cab to arrive. The flakes of snow were growing more frequent, although they were still sparse enough to remain separate on the pavement before her. A car slowed and stopped. It was an old car, some kind of Peugeot, and not well maintained. The driver, a young Asian man, got out.

'You the cab for Paddington?' he asked her. Janet had to say yes, although the state of the car gave her pause. She was slightly worried about inhaling fully once inside, in case there were any distressing smells, but she saw that there was a little traffic-light air freshener hanging from the rearview mirror and risked it. The smell was musty, but not distressing.

The roads were no freer than they had been an hour before.

'You take a train?' asked the driver, smiling into the rearview mirror.

'That's right,' Janet replied, discouragingly.

'What time?' he asked.

'No particular time,' she said. Then, glancing to meet his eye in the mirror, she added 'as soon as possible', just in case he assumed he need make no effort to get her to the station.

The driver grinned at her again and Janet looked away, out of the window. He was quite handsome, although he was far too thin and had an unsuccessful moustache, possibly grown, Janet thought, to conceal a weak mouth. He seemed inclined to talk, despite her lack of response, and between central Ealing and the Hanger Lane gyratory system ventured several details about his life in Whitechapel with his wife and children. Janet couldn't make much of this, as she found his accent almost impenetrable. There were just random words, 'kids' or 'house', to anchor meaning. She nodded as though she understood, wishing herself home.

The snow was now coming down heavily. It made Janet's eyes hurt to follow the procession of flakes, like static on a TV screen, but she felt compelled to watch them again as soon as she had looked away. And besides, she felt more comfortable with her gaze away from the car's interior.

Although she no longer felt a trace of the dizziness to which she had succumbed at Selfridges, Janet was overwhelmed by tiredness. Heat blew at her, the seat was soft, and soon she was asleep. A fraction of her consciousness remained tethered to the sound of the engine, but she was otherwise buoyed by eddying associations striving to be dreams. She attempted to post a coffeemaker through Tina's letterbox, and was caught in the act by Father Christmas, who turned out to be trying to sell her something. Then she was crimping the crusts on an apple pie, while her mother opined that she hadn't made enough for everyone. Janet was arguing with her when she woke. The driver was saying something.

'I beg your pardon?' she said crossly. Her mouth felt dry, and she was annoyed to think that it had been gaping open as she slept, in full view of the driver. She then realised that they had stopped.

'I just go to look at the engine,' the driver smiled at her. From the window, Janet saw the snow swirling thickly, so thickly that a dirty rime of it had accumulated on the road, despite the passage of traffic. They were nowhere familiar to her. The car had pulled in on a dual carriageway bordered by depressed suburban houses.

'This isn't Paddington,' she protested, but the driver was already out of the car, lifting the bonnet. Janet could feel her heart punching through her breastbone. They could be any-where. You heard all sorts of stories, terrible things that happened. She craned to see if there was a phone box in view. Maybe she could slip out while he was preoccupied by the engine and phone the police. Or just catch a passer-by. But there was no phone box and not a person in sight. She might slip in the snow and hurt herself – her shoes had a heel. And any attempt to escape might incense the driver into an extravagant act of violence.

Of course, she tried to admonish herself, there might be nothing at all to worry about. He could be perfectly harm-less. Janet wondered at what point she would know this. Stealthily, she felt in her handbag for anything suitable as a weapon, her blind fingers moving gently so that the driver would not be alerted if he turned to see her. She had a man-icure case, containing a variety of implements. She gradually unzipped it, and inched out her nail scissors. She wondered if she would be capable of using them. When Tina was tiny, a simple boy from the village had lifted her out of her pram while Janet was in the post office. Janet had run out and clawed her nails across his face, screaming, as she retrieved the chuckling baby. Afterwards, people had told her that the boy would never have done Tina any harm. She still felt guilty when she thought about it.

The driver came back to the car, vibrating his lips and rubbing his hands together in an ingratiating stereotype of a man exposed to the cold. His short leather jacket was probably a plastic imitation. It looked thin, and didn't fit him properly.

'It's no good, innit,' the driver shouted through the shut window, ever smiling, the weakness of his mouth revealed. 'I'll have to ring the recovery, lady.'

'Where are we?' Janet asked, attempting a neutral tone.

'The North Circular, innit,' the driver told her.

'You must have got lost,' Janet said.

His smile was pure apology, overdone. 'Very sorry. Bad weather.' He leaned in to the door. 'I'll find a phone.'

Janet relaxed her grip on the palmed pair of scissors as he moved away from the car. He spoke to her, but she didn't hear what he said. He turned back to her, knocked on her window. She edged away. Now, this was the moment. He opened her door, which she had thought locked. His breath plumed into her face.

'I said, you better keep warm—' he started, grinning. But she was already flailing at him with the closed blades of the tiny scissors, and his grin stopped in amazement. The scissors caught him at the base of the neck, and stuck there, even when Janet released them. The driver tried to shout, but it turned thin, like a scream. Perhaps it was a scream.

'What the fuck—'

He was scrambling for her. Janet backed into the other door, fumbled it open. And then she was skidding along the snowy embankment by the side of the road, intent on a pedestrian bridge a couple of hundred yards in front of her. She didn't look back. Her handbag slapped at her hip, compromising her balance. The cold sliced at her lungs and her vision was hazed by the snow. She was panting. Climbing the stairs of the bridge, she realised she had left her new coat in the car. But she would tell the police, when she got to them. She concentrated on keeping her footing. If they needed proof, she had the receipt folded into her purse, she was sure she had. It wasn't the sort of thing she slipped up on. Her own ragged breath muffled the traffic sounds as she crossed the bridge. Not much further, labouring now to keep going. Then, at last, she was there. Safe. Thankfully, she descended the last few steps and skittered to the other side of the road, where a dingy parade of shops signalled the start of civilisation.

Twinkle

People grow apart. It's one of those truths, disguised as a cliché. For example: where I live there are three dry-cleaners on the road I have to walk down to get to the tube station. I always used to take my dry-cleaning into the last dry-cleaner before the station. I don't know why, I just liked the look of it more than the other two. Maybe the colour of the sign. Yellow. Anyway, then I didn't really feel like taking my dry-cleaning into the yellow dry-cleaner any more. There was nothing wrong with the quality of their cleaning; I'd just gone off them. I fancied a change. Which is my point: if you can feel that way about a dry-cleaner, it's hardly surprising that you can grow apart from someone you've spent the larger part of your life with, is there?

This isn't a romantic thing, before you get the wrong idea. It's way more bizarre than that. The thing is, I'm in a manner of speaking being stalked. It started in the library. I'm between jobs at the moment, and going to the library is something I do at least once a week, partly because it's free, and partly because it adds an important sense of structure to my life. They also have an excellent video collection, which I use far more than the books part. So. I'm in the library. *The Wages of Fear*, *The Discreet Charm of the Bourgeoisie*, maybe *Beaches* again. I become aware of someone watching me, or more likely I just look up and see the woman staring at me. She doesn't even pretend not to be staring when I stare back at her. She gives a shy, excited little wave.

I definitely, definitely do not know this woman. I would have remembered, because she's certainly distinctive. She's around my age, but she's wearing her very blonde hair in a large pink bow on top of her head. On me, it might be kooky, although I'm just beginning to be sensitive to the mutton-dressing-up-as implications of that sort of thing, but on her it just looks odd. And she's wearing a dinky little pseudo-Prada schoolgirl outfit, with a neat little three-buttoned coat over a neat little skirt, and T-bar shoes and white ankle socks. All of which could be funky, but it's way too clinical on her. She's got round blue eyes that beam friendliness, and it's when I see them that I decide she's a nutter. Before she can make her way over from the biography section, I skedaddle. I'm just not in the mood.

Then I'm in the chemist's dawdling over shampoo brands and this time she says hello. There's no escape.

'Hello, Sarah Marie!'

I say hello back, smiling, because you never know. It is possible to forget people, although I'm still pretty sure she's a stranger. Although she knows my middle name, which of course I never use (middle names are the foot spas of names; consigned to uselessness the moment you get them). And I certainly don't use it professionally, which is my other thought: that maybe she's recognised me from the TV, which can happen from time to time. But the advert hasn't been on for months, which is one of the reasons I'm balking at premium prices for the shampoo which will restore body and shine to my damaged, dry or processed hair. No one has called me Sarah Marie since. Well. No one has ever called me Sarah Marie really, although it is technically correct.

'How are you?' she continues. She has a large head for her body, I notice. It is this, along with the clothes, that makes you think she's away with the fairies. I say I'm fine, although in a bit of a hurry. I ask her how she is, giving it a lot of sub-textual, hurried distraction. I imagine a child at home, with a sore throat, and possibly a temperature. I have left it to come and buy nostrums. Nostra? The woman tips her head to one side and smiles, winsomely.

'You don't remember who I am, do you, Sarah Marie?' she says. I stretch my smile and make it a good one, implying great charm marred by random blots of absent-mindedness.

'Twinkle,' she smiles, with gentle reproach. Twinkle. You'd think this would do it. But it elicits nothing.

'Twinkle!' I give it an octave, apologetic-cum-warm-cum-I-remember-now. 'How are you?'

Her smile, I have to say, is rather enchanting. Seeing it, I am beginning to feel a stirring of familiarity, completely unanchored by any specific memory.

'Oh I'm very well,' Twinkle says dismissively. 'But how are you?'

She really seems to want to know, so I tell her. I almost don't go into detail about my recent hideous experience with a theatre-in-education tour of *The Hobbit*, but she gets it out of me. We must be standing in Boots for ten minutes while I give her chapter and verse on the current state of my life, professional and personal.

After I tear myself away I think no more about it, as you don't. But I see Twinkle around after this, out and about. She has obviously moved into the area. And she's always keen to chat, although she's not much of a talker herself. Gradually, things she says like 'You were always very determined', or 'I knew you'd be famous one day!' make me decide that we must have known each other when we were kids. Her memory is obviously phenomenal, compared to mine. I do have a blurred recollection of a birthday party, and some jam tarts, and I connect Twinkle with this event, although I don't dare to bring it up, in case I'm wrong. Obviously, seeing her makes me slightly uncomfortable, because I always think she's going to find out how little I do remember, and be hurt by it. Nobody enjoys being forgotten, even if you were five years old when you last met. It's human nature, isn't it? Like people forgetting your name. I hate that.

So far though, it isn't worrying. It only starts to be worrying when I turn up for the audition. This is for an all-female profit-share production of *Journey's End*, and my agent has put me up for the lead, the public school hero (now heroine, obviously), Stanhope. The director's idea is to do the whole thing as a sort of Angela Brazil type parody of imperialism, as though we're girls doing *Journey's End* as a school play. This idea hums, in my opinion. But it's a while since I've auditioned for anything, and my agent thinks that this director, who is called Lucy, known as Loose, is on her way to being hot. And she could be right, so I go along, even though I don't see how you can be hot by coming up with ideas about sending up an ancient play that would be a commentary on imperialism even if you did it straight, using a framing device that is in itself outdated. I mean, is anyone now saying that the First World War was a good thing? But Loose, not me, is the one who's hot. As my agent reminds me.

The auditions are in the theatre, which is above a pub, like lots of good spaces. I see a couple of people I know, which is both reassuring and depressing. Reassuring, because I know I can act them off this or any stage. Depressing, because if they get a part and I don't, this will mean that in the eyes of the world they're better actors than I am, and I think they're crap, so this will mean that I'm definitively crap. And one of them's lost a lot of weight.

Loose herself is a terrifying figure. She looks tortured and hollowed-out and medieval, like a junkie Virgin Mary, and she's wearing a little woolly cap. She never smiles, which of course means I will do the smiling for both of us when we have to talk. I hate that, but there's no way I'm going to be able to stop myself smiling. I'm more than nervous, even if I don't give a stuff about the play. There are three people due to read before me, as they are, of course, running late. I have to wait in the pub downstairs until they call me, which means I'll have even longer than anticipated to be paralysed with nerves. Terrific.

This is the freaky thing. When I go down into the pub, Twinkle is there, sitting on a stool at the bar, swinging her legs and sipping a pineapple juice.

'Hello, Sarah Marie,' she says in her friendly way. Her being in the pub is more than a coincidence – I've taken two buses to get here. She smiles at me.

'You said you had an audition,' she explains, quite openly. It's true, I had mentioned it when we last bumped into each other outside the supermarket. She got it out of me, I don't know how. She's just such a good listener. For one paranoid moment I think that she's muscling in on the job. I don't actually know what Twinkle does for a living, after all. It's not beyond the realms of possibility that she's an actress – she certainly seems to have enough free time.

'Why are you here?' I ask. On the nose. You couldn't get away with it in a play. Twinkle puts down her pineapple juice and sucks the moisture transferred from the outside of the glass off her fingers.

'I thought you might be nervous,' she says. 'You know how you get. Think of the Nativity play.'

The Nativity play. I was sick before I went on. They ripped off my cotton-wool beard as I stood over the toilet and got a boy (Christopher Butterfield, in case you're interested) to go on as the innkeeper instead. When I began to feel better I behaved badly about it. But this was a very long time ago.

'I do do this as a living,' I tell her, aiming for lofty dignity. Twinkle pats my hand and offers to buy me a drink. Although I'm basically pissed off that she's as good as followed me to the audition, I don't have the gumption to show her that I'm pissed off, so I accept the drink. And the thing is, having her there does take my mind off things, actually. I tell her about the other people who have turned up and it calms me down. In the end I do a blinding audition. That's not boasting. Every once in a while, you know you're good.

But it's getting tricky, the whole Twinkle thing. I can't help feeling that it's gone beyond the nipping-it-in-the-bud stage. I'm going to have to get a bloody great set of secateurs and prune her out of my life before she runs rampant. For example. A couple of times she's even come with me on the bus to rehearsals. When I try to suggest as discreetly as possible that this is (a) unnecessary and (b) weird, she just gives me her round-eyed smile and says it's no trouble. And actually, when I'm with her I do quite enjoy her company. It's not like she makes any demands on me. It's only afterwards, when I think about it, that it makes my flesh crawl a bit. Because let's face it, her life must be pretty empty if she's got nothing better to do than follow me around. Emptier than mine, even. Ha ha.

Although, with the play, I mustn't grumble. Must not complain. Loose is still terrifying, but the rest of the cast are a laugh. The stage manager's got a broad chest and naughty eyes, and he and I are doing some serious flirting, which is good for the soul and other parts. So life could be a lot worse, really. My only source of complaint, apart from the

Twinkle phenomenon, is in the sleep department. I'm usually like the proverbial (but not actual, I've noticed) baby, but for a couple of nights I've woken up with a sharp sort of stabbing pain in my side. At first I thought it was appendicitis, but I looked it up in the medical dictionary at the library and it's on the wrong side. Further reading has persuaded me that it might be sciatica, and once the dress rehearsal is out of the way I'm booking myself in for a session with the acupuncturist. Could be a chakra blockage, pure and simple. It doesn't last long, anyway, even when it wakes me up.

As part of the rehearsal process, Loose forces us all to take a trip to the Imperial War Museum so that some spoddy bloke there can lecture us on war being hell and trench foot and other details which will add texture to our performances. Quite how the Angela Brazil thing works in with this I am unsure, but I'm no troublemaker. Shut up and drink the Koolaid, that's my motto. You can imagine how I feel when we get to the museum and all pile out of Loose's vintage Skoda and I see Twinkle waiting for me at the entrance. Picture the embarrassment of being greeted as Sarah Marie, for a start. Loose and the cast are clearly very curious about her. If they had thought bubbles, you would read 'Who is this eccentrically groomed stranger?' floating above their heads. I tell them I'll join them in a minute.

'Look Twinkle—' I begin, pulling her off to one side. Her eyes widen at my tone.

'Is something wrong, Sarah Marie?' she asks.

'It's not that I don't like you,' I begin, hoping that she'll interrupt. She doesn't. I continue. 'It's not that I don't like you – Twinkle – but I'm concerned that well, maybe I've got this wrong, you know, in which case – but you seem to be following me.'

She nods placidly. She's not even going to disagree with me. I'm sweating.

'Well, I'd prefer it if you didn't. Sorry.'

She smiles.

'OK,' she says. And she turns round and walks down the steps and away. That's it. It's not even a gesture, like it would be if I were doing the walking away. She really doesn't seem to mind. By this point I'm actually shaking. If truth be told, I'm more sensitive than I look. And I've seen enough films, haven't we all, to wonder if her apparently calm exit isn't going to have some kind of gory pay-off, along pet-boiling lines.

All of which is probably the reason that I don't, according to Loose, give the afternoon session my all. Pulling me aside to tell me this, she not only gets on my tits but as far as I'm concerned, jumps up and down and does a spot of rhythmic gymnastics while she's in the neighbourhood. How can she tell that my sensory visualisation of the symptoms of mustard-gas poisoning is less committed than that of any other member of the cast? But that's what she accuses me of, fixing me with her solemn smack-head Madonna stare beneath the woolly cap.

'Wow. I'm sorry you think that, Loose,' I tell her. 'Because – God – I really felt as though I was giving it a hundred per cent.'

Of course it only occurs to me later that she fancies Mr Naughty Eyes as well. So I handle it in entirely the wrong

way by getting a bit chippy and asking about the whole
Angela Brazil thing, unsupported by any of the others even
though they've bitched about it to me privately often
enough when Loose hasn't been around.

'If we're schoolgirls acting at being soldiers,' I say, fatally,
'shouldn't we be doing visualisations of being schoolgirls?'

By the time we leave the museum, Loose wants a private
chat. In other words, she's firing me. She actually uses the
expression creative differences. I wish I had the courage to
pull the rim of her woolly cap over her beautiful, agonised
face, but because I don't have the courage, I burst into tears
instead. She offers to give me a lift back in the Skoda but
essentially I run away. I try to pretend that I'm meeting a
friend but this doesn't fool anyone.

Twinkle is at the bus stop. Naturally. The pink bow, the
happy-happy smile. This is all I need.

'Stop fucking following me!' I scream at her. 'Get your
own fucking life!'

She offers me a handkerchief. Not a tissue, a handkerchief, folded with a pink border.

'Are you all right, Sarah Marie?' she says.

'No I'm not!' I'm really yelling. Other people at the bus
stop are edging away as much as is possible while still officially waiting for a bus. 'I am not all right. And it's none of
your business! I am not five years old. You are not my
friend. I don't even know you, OK? I might have once, but
people change!'

I stamp away from the bus stop, without turning back to
see how Twinkle has taken all this. All the way, I half expect
her to catch up with me, but she doesn't.

I get home wet, because it starts raining and naturally I don't have an umbrella. While I'm peeling off my disgusting jumper, which reeks of old ladies because I got it from a charity shop and water activates its historic smell, the phone rings. Thank God, it's my mother. When I say thank God you can tell what a state I'm in. At least it isn't Adolf Hitler, Loose or Twinkle. Mum only has to ask me how I am and I'm ready to howl again. I'm hoping that she'll be nasty to me so that I have an excuse to shout at her, but much more distressingly, she's in one of her odd moods where she suddenly reveals that she's actually been listening to what I've said in our last three conversations. For example.

'How's the profit share going?' she asks.

This from the woman who, when I was appearing in a tour of *The Wild Duck*, turned up to a performance and swore blind that I'd told her it was a musical. I try to change the subject, but she's tenacious. Finally, I have to admit that I've resigned from the production.

'There were creative differences,' I tell her. She sighs, and tells me a long story about a grievance she has with a neighbour, involving some old curtains. Listening to my mother's anecdotes is like trying to concentrate on a weather report. You drift off during the bit about a warm front, it gets to the end and you realise that you haven't taken in a single detail. Fortunately, she never notices.

'Mum,' I interrupt her, before she can embark on another one. 'Can you remember a girl I was at school with when I was little, called Twinkle?'

She laughs. 'Oh I remember Twinkle all right,' she says

indulgently. 'Your dad used to be frightened of her, don't you remember?'

'No,' I say. 'That's why I'm asking.'

'He used to say to me, she seems that convinced.'

I persist. 'What about?'

'You were such a funny little thing,' she sighs. 'You know, if I gave you a biscuit: "Twinkle wants one too", you'd always say. So you'd get two.'

'Didn't Twinkle like biscuits?' I ask.

'It's amazing what you grow out of,' muses Mum. 'I think a lot of children make things up at that age.'

'Make things up?'

'Yes, you know. Have imaginary friends.'

Mum sticks to her story. As we speak, I neck some vodka from the bottle in the freezer and try yoga breathing to slow my pulse. It was definitely Twinkle, Mum says. She's always remembered because it was such an unusual name.

'And there was the witch, of course,' she has to continue.

'What witch?'

She gives another little sigh. Fond, though.

'It's amazing what you don't remember. The witch who lived by your bed and woke you up. She pinched your side whenever—'

I stop the conversation right there.

Cinderella

It's not that I'm not into Adam, because I am, totally. But sometimes when we do it I pretend he's someone else. I keep my eyes open and it's still his face, but it belongs to someone completely different. Not anyone in particular, just different. It sends me. He thinks it's what he's doing. He smiles. It's a bit like when I was little and I'd stare at something, like a dandelion, and do something with my eyes so that they almost crossed but didn't, and when I managed to do it properly it was like a click and I wasn't looking at the dandelion any more. I mean I was, but I wasn't. Like drugs.

I do the same thing when I'm bored at work. Like, I'll look at the pattern on a shirt and try the click. Only when the shop's really quiet because otherwise people are going to think you're a right nonce with that look on your face. The manager, Kay, she'd give me a bollocking if she caught me. Not shouting, she's just really sarcastic and makes you feel like an idiot. With a big bum. Sometimes when I go into the back for my break I hear her and Denise giggling behind me. I've got a big arse, no two ways about it.

I work in Kookaï. It's all right. I like meeting people. If I'd been brainy at school I'd have tried to be an air hostess or a travel courier, but you have to be good at languages. My older sister, Chrissie, she's only been abroad once, to Greece, and she didn't like it, but I love it. I've been abroad loads of times, including when I was five with my mum and dad, which was the time Chrissie went as well. Mum won a competition. Fred was surprised that I'd been to Spain three times. He wanted me to speak Spanish to him but I told him to piss off because I knew he was only asking so that he could laugh at me. I'm not stupid, even if I look it. I tell him that. He puts on this serious look and says 'Caterina, I know you are a very intelligent person.'

I told Fred that my first name was really Catherine and now he always calls me Caterina even though everyone else calls me Jo. The only reason Joanna isn't first on my birth certificate is because my dad was obsessed with us all having names beginning with C. Him, Colin, my mum, Cynthia, Christina, Christopher and me. But from day one everyone's called me Jo or Joanna. Except Fred.

He came into the shop last thing one Friday. It's later opening so lots of girls come in after work to get something new for going out. He looked a bit dodgy, this old bloke, going through rails of clothes. He said that he was looking for a dress as a present for a friend of his who was my size, and could I help? Obvious or what. He held up this tarty-looking dress and asked me what I thought of it.

'Quite honestly,' I said, 'if you gave that to me as a present I'd throw it back in your face.'

He put it back. I picked out a couple of things and he asked me to try them on. Kay was giving me funny looks by then and I said I couldn't. I held the clothes up against me so that he could get a rough idea of what they'd look like if I'd actually been wearing them. He took everything to the counter without even looking at the price tags.

He said he was visiting from Spain and his name was Fred. For Federico. You have to put the r in for it to sound right short. He asked me my name and said he'd like to buy me a dress as a thank-you for my help. Sod it, I thought. He had a massive gold watch on and a flash suit. When he opened his wallet it was wall-to-wall credit cards. There was this dress. It'd come into the shop a couple of days ago and I'd thought of buying it even though it was on the pricey side. I put it on the pile and Fred paid for it without batting an eyelid. Then he wanted my phone number.

'I've got a boyfriend,' I told him. Fred smiled and said that coming from Spain he didn't know many people and that he just liked talking to new people and that I seemed a friendly and interesting person. Kay was listening to this and giving me looks that I was sure he could see, ignorant cow. She narked me so much I told Fred that he could meet me the next day at this café I sometimes go to on my dinner hour. When he left he handed me the bag with my new dress in it and did a little bow with his head. I could tell Kay was jealous.

I wore the dress when I went out with Adam that night. He said I looked nice when I asked him what he thought of it. We just went out for a drink, then back to his flat as usual. Chrissie hasn't said anything about not wanting me to bring people back but it feels funny with her kids there and everything, and I don't like being round Nick, her husband, with a boyfriend. There's just as many people round at Adam's but he shares with other students and anyway his room's five times the size of mine. Adam's from London, Blackheath, so he could live at home but he said he'd wanted to move out when he started college. Once I asked him what his dad did and he said it was irrelevant to our relationship, and why did I want to know. Just nosy, I said. We haven't been going out that long. He's doing a BA Honours degree in Communication Studies.

Adam's got beautiful hair. I mean I fancy him all over but I love to look at his hair and stroke it. It's what some people call dirty blond but there's nothing dirty about it, it shines. He pushes his hand up through it when he's talking and it sticks out from his head in a spike for a couple of seconds, then it falls apart and back to his head slowly, like toffee-coloured feathers. Rich boy's hair. I don't say that to him because he doesn't like me going on about him having money. He's never actually said he's rich, but I know. Things like he's got a really nice leather jacket, second hand, but really good second hand, and loads of CDs and he said something once that I worked out meant he'd had a credit card since he was sixteen. And his duvet. It's a double one and it's really warm and thick but it sits on you like air. I've got a duvet at Chrissie's that I brought from home and it

feels nothing like his. It's got lumps, and when it's cold I
have to put a blanket on top.

'It's brilliant, your duvet,' I said to him that night when
we were pulling it round us. He looked at me like I was a
mong.

I'd sort of forgotten about seeing Fred the next day
until it was my dinner hour. I didn't really think he'd turn
up, actually. But he was sitting there in the café, suit and
all, with all these people round him eating fry-ups. It
made me want to laugh when I saw him. He stood up and
kissed me on one cheek, then the other. I felt a bit embarrassed.

I slid into the seat opposite him – it's one of those plastic
booths that makes farting noises if you bounce across it
instead of sliding. There was a watch on the table in front of
me, laid out with its strap undone.

'I notice you don't wear a watch,' said Fred. 'Maybe that's
why you are late.'

I don't wear a watch because my last one fell off my wrist
somewhere when the strap broke. It broke because it was
crappy plastic, like all my watches. The watch that Fred
was trying to give me was a proper metal one. In fact it
looked like gold.

'Please take it,' he said.

'I can't,' I told him.

'What is the problem? I want to make a gift to you. I am
a wealthy man, this means very little to me.'

'Really, I can't wear it.'

'You are worried your boyfriend will see?'

'No, I can't wear gold.'

I explained that I'm a winter, so I can only wear silver. Chrissie's friend Mish did my colours and I'm a deep winter. We're the only group that can wear black, although most women do, even clear springs who look really washed out in it. But being a deep winter means gold jewellery is definitely out. Fred took the watch back and said he'd get me another one. I felt all right about that. It wasn't like I'd asked him for it in the first place.

He bought me my dinner. Lunch. He didn't eat anything but he smoked and had two coffees. I was starving – I ordered their all-day breakfast plate with the eggs they scramble through the cappuccino machine.

'So what about this boyfriend of yours?' Fred asked when I was waiting for my food. I cadged a fag off him and stretched the truth a bit by telling him that we'd been going out for three years and we were engaged. It seemed like the best way of him not getting the wrong idea. I mean if Adam had walked in I'd've felt really bad, not because anything was going on, but just because of the way it looked. Fred wanted to know when he could see me again, to give me the watch. I told him not for a week, I was busy. He said he was going to France on business.

'Next time,' he said, 'come to a flat I have. It is better than this place.'

He wrote the address down for me on a card. It was on Park Lane. I wasn't sure where Park Lane was, it's one of those bits of London I only know from the Monopoly board. I hadn't definitely decided to go to this flat, but thinking about it didn't worry me. It was something to do with Fred's feet. They were small, and he wore these naff slip-on shoes with pointed toes and tassels and a sort of woven leather pattern on top. They probably cost a fortune, but they made me feel sorry for him.

That night, me and Adam passed a jewellery shop on the way to the pub. I stopped to look at watches in the window, seeing if there were any like the one Fred had tried to give me, with the price on. Adam moaned that he was freezing his bollocks off.

'Do I wear a watch?' I asked him. I pulled my jacket sleeve over my hand so he couldn't cheat. When we'd just started going out I put my hand over my face and asked him what colour my eyes were. He got it wrong.

'No,' he said. I think it was a guess. I pulled my sleeve back to show him my bare arm. Adam joined his thumb and middle finger round my wrist, like a bracelet. There was room to spare. He kissed me.

He was being really nice, like he can be. Other times it's like me when I do the click thing, but I don't do it when we're supposed to be having a conversation. And that's when he's not on anything. Parties and that, there's no point pretending he's a normal human being. I just leave him to it. But when he's in a good mood like this he's perfect. He lets me stroke his hair. Other times he pulls away. I don't know why I didn't tell him about Fred. There were probably loads of things he didn't tell me, anyway.

'What about me?' he said.

'What about you?'

'Do I wear a watch?'

'No.' I knew he didn't. I tried to put my thumb and finger round his wrist but they barely got round half way. I had to use both hands to make a bracelet. Adam thought this was hilarious. He said my hands were tragically small.

At work that week Kay asked 'How's the sugar daddy?' I just blanked her. When she went off on her break I got Fred's card out of my purse and tore it up into the bin. Then I thought of Kay finding the bits so I picked them out of the rubbish and put them back in my bag.

On Friday night, a mate of Adam's was playing in this band at a club. Adam was in a mood and once we got there he went off with his mates from college and acted like I didn't exist. I didn't know anyone else. The band was crap as well, and the beer was really expensive. After about an hour of it I told Adam I was going home. I could tell he was surprised, because usually even if I'm having a bad time I wait until he's ready to leave. He might have gone with me if his mates hadn't been there but he had to look cool in front of them. Up till then I would have just gone back to Chrissie's but he was being such a prick. I looked through my purse and found the torn-up bits of Fred's card. I'd forgotten to get rid of them – you know what it's like at the bottom of your bag. I rang the number, really expecting no one to be there. I suppose I was just pissed off with Adam. I could see him from the phone, showing his mates a pathetic trick with a beer mat.

Fred was in. He even recognised my voice. He said to get in a taxi and he'd pay at the other end. Sod it, I thought. I'd never taken a proper taxi just on my own, without anyone to split the fare. I was glad Fred was paying, since it came to nearly twenty quid.

The flat was amazing. It was twice the size of Chrissie's

house, but all on one floor. I was busting for a pee when I got there because of the beer at the club and coming back from the toilet I couldn't find the living room straight away because there were too many doors. I felt a right nonce by the time I got back, but Fred didn't say anything. He was sitting on a huge settee, just waiting for me, not watching TV or reading the paper or anything. There wasn't even any music on. The settee was so big that he had to sit at the edge of it so that his feet could touch the ground, like a little boy.

The flat didn't look like a man's. You could say that the living room was clear spring, which was wrong for Fred because he was a deep winter like me, black hair and nearly black eyes. But there was this shiny stuff on the walls, like satin on the inside of a jewellery box I had when I was little. The same blue was in the curtain material, covered with pink squiggles. The curtains were all messed about with, with dips in them and tassels and cord and everything, and there were lots of shiny hard lemon and pink coloured cushions, like sherbet sweets. It was all a bit much, really. The carpet was beautiful though. If it had been me on my own I'd have stretched out on the carpet and just stroked it and rolled around on it. I slipped one of my shoes off and I could feel how soft and thick it was under my toes, even with tights on. Like one of those special cats. Persians.

Fred asked me what I wanted to drink. I said champagne, just to try it on, and he'd actually got some. I'd really rather have had a beer. Anyway, I didn't want to drink that much because I knew he was probably trying to get me drunk.

When he brought me the champagne he gave me a box with a silver watch in it. It wasn't exactly what I'd have chosen myself but I didn't want to hurt his feelings.

'Allow me,' he said, and took it out of the box and put it on my wrist.

'You have no ring,' he said.

I didn't know what he meant, because I was wearing a couple of rings, then I realised he meant no engagement ring. I'd forgotten about telling him me and Adam were engaged. I said that we were both saving up so that we could afford a proper one. He had this look on his face like that was the worst thing in the world he could think of.

'Before you say it, that's something you can't buy me,' I said. He didn't laugh. He didn't laugh or smile much at all. Although he wasn't sad or anything.

I asked Fred if his wife had decorated the flat, half to see if he was married. He said no, he didn't have a wife. He could have been lying. He didn't wear a wedding ring. I couldn't tell how old he was, fifty-odd, maybe. Definitely older than my dad. He said that this was just one of the properties he owned in London. His real home was in Barcelona. He asked where I lived and I told him about moving down to London and living with Chrissie and Nick. He looked even worse than he had when I said about the engagement ring.

'Caterina,' he said, 'I have many properties in London that are completely empty. It would be a favour to me if you moved into one of them. Please think about it. All over London. Think of an area you'd like to live.'

He could see I was looking iffy at this. He said please just to think about it. No pressure. He said that a lot: no pressure. He took out a key ring with loads of keys on it and pulled one off and put it on the coffee table in front of me.

'Please, this is the spare key to this flat. I am often away, so if you ever need to stay here—'

'I don't think so, Fred—'

'Please.'

I didn't take the key. He wasn't narked or anything, but he left it there on the table. I said I thought I'd better be going, and he said he'd call me a cab. While we were waiting for it, we ran out of things to say.

'Know any jokes?' I said, just to be funny. He said he only knew Spanish jokes. He asked if I knew any. Chrissie's Nick is always telling jokes and he says I've got no sense of humour because I never laugh.

'Knock knock,' I said, remembering one. Then I realised Fred didn't know what to say next.

'You're supposed to say "who's there?",' I explained. He wanted to know why.

'You just do,' I said. I had to think about why. 'It's like I'm knocking on your door and you want to know who it is.'

'This is a joke?' He wasn't getting at me, he was confused.

'Forget it,' I said.

'No, please, it is interesting to me.'

'Knock knock.'

'Who is there?'

'Doctor.' I knew he wasn't going to say anything. 'And you say doctor who . . .'

'Doctor who?'

Then I remembered that's the end of the joke. The joke is getting the person to say Doctor Who. I tried to explain this to Fred, I mean it was never a funny joke or anything, if you think about knock knock jokes, no one's ever laughed at them. But Fred was excited when I started to explain about Doctor Who. He used to watch it all the time in Spain. He liked the one with the long scarf best, he said. He did a dalek voice, but saying something in Spanish and it was the first time I'd seen him laugh. Then the cab arrived and Fred wanted to know when he could see me again. I felt freaked out about him expecting it, like a regular thing. Also, he kissed my hand when he said goodbye, which really gave me the creeps.

'I'm not going to sleep with you, Fred,' I told him.

'I know this. No pressure. We are friends.'

He kissed me on each cheek and pushed a note in my hand. It was a fifty-pound note. He said it was for the cab. There was no point in arguing. In fact when we got back to Chrissie's the cab driver said he didn't have change so I ended up using my own money.

When I got in I hid the watch Fred had given me in a drawer, then the next morning I thought I was being stupid and took it out and put it on again. If Adam noticed it I'd say it was a birthday present from my mum and dad and it was late because they'd had to have the strap altered to fit me properly. If Chrissie noticed it I'd say it was a present from Adam. Chrissie noticed it, Adam didn't.

I decided I wouldn't see Fred again. I couldn't find anything I liked to spend the fifty pounds on, and I felt funny about it, so I used it to take Adam out for dinner on

Saturday night. We had a really nice Italian with loads of wine and there was still some money left. I said I'd got a bonus at work. Adam said any time I wanted to treat him was fine by him. He was being perfect.

I used the change from the meal to pay for a taxi back to Adam's flat. With all the wine I was all over him and we were practically doing it in the back seat by the time the cab stopped. We charged straight for Adam's bedroom when we got in, but one of the other students, Dink, stopped us on the way to tell Adam his mum had rung and wanted to know what time she could expect him for lunch. The way Dink said it you could tell Adam's mum had kept her talking for hours.

When we got into Adam's room we didn't even make it to the mattress the first time. After the second time I fell straight to sleep.

Sundays are difficult because Adam sometimes has to do an essay and even if I'm really quiet he says that he can't concentrate when I'm there in the room. I don't like to hang round Chrissie's too much because she and Nick usually seem to end up rowing. I half wished I'd taken the key to his flat off Fred. I thought of all those empty rooms, and the carpet. Adam was miserable about his mum and dad expecting him home for lunch. I tried to cheer him up and he said I didn't know what they were like and I said I'd like to meet them.

'No you wouldn't,' he said. I asked if I could stay in his room until he got back since he wouldn't be using it. I even offered to do some tidying up. He put his hand round my wrist and slid it up and down my arm, over Fred's watch.

'You can come home with me if you like,' he said. I knew it wasn't a real invitation because his parents hadn't asked me. I said that. He said it didn't matter.

'Do they even know about me?' I asked.

'Sort of,' he said.

Their house was gorgeous, not as flash as Fred's but everything like you see in magazines and on TV, more my taste. The kitchen had loads of wood and weird things hanging up like more complicated cheese graters and stuff so that it was quite untidy but you knew everything was expensive. Mr and Mrs Flynn were like that as well. Classy, but not in a snobby way. They said to call them Adrian and Jenny but I felt embarrassed and managed not to have to call them anything. Adam did his click thing and the more questions they asked him the less he said, but his mum and dad both talked a lot and seemed not to notice. They asked me a lot of questions as well and Mr Flynn seemed interested in things like what sort of training I got at Kookaï. There was tons to eat, then Adam's mum brought in a fruit pavlova with candles stuck in it and she and Mr Flynn started singing Happy Birthday. I joined in, but I was surprised.

'You didn't tell me it was your birthday,' I said after we'd finished.

'Oh Adam,' said Mrs Flynn, and Mr Flynn said something about Adam being a man of mystery. Adam just pushed his hand through his hair so that it spiked. His mum passed him an envelope. It had a card in it and also a cheque, although I couldn't see for how much. He kissed his mum and said thank you and then kissed his dad which made them both a bit embarrassed.

'We thought you could choose what you wanted,' said Mr Flynn. 'No point pretending we can fathom your tastes these days.'

I wanted to help wash up but Mrs Flynn said it all went into the machine anyway and for Adam to show me round the garden.

'Why?' said Adam. But I said I'd like to see, to be polite. He took me outside. It was a big garden, very tidy. I don't know anything about flowers, I couldn't even tell you the names of trees. From the lawn we could see his mum and dad through the kitchen window, watching. They waved at us. We waved back.

'Fucking hell,' said Adam. We turned to face away from the house, getting the giggles. 'I told you,' he said. I said I thought they were really nice.

'You look like your mum,' I told him. They both had the same mouth, sort of curly.

'I'm adopted,' he said. He'd never told me that. It was hard to think what to say. I tried to pull a leaf off a tree but it wouldn't come away.

'I'm special because they chose me,' said Adam, imitating something they'd said to him.

I let go of the branch and it nearly whipped him in the eye.

'Well, it's true, isn't it? If someone like, chooses you, it's because of you, not just what they end up with.'

He used his heel to hack at the edge of the lawn, where a flowerbed started.

'Actually, it's because of them, if you bother thinking about it. They don't know anything about you actually.'

'Oh is it, actually?'

For something to do, I asked if I could see his room. It was at the top of the house, with big windows. There were things in the room that I couldn't believe Adam was ever interested in, but there they were, like model cars lined up on a shelf over his bed in order from biggest to littlest, and a collection of *Star Trek* figures. He started kissing me. I said his parents might come in but it just made him hornier. He pushed me down on to the bed. I was still telling him to get off, half joking and half serious, but he wasn't listening. Sod it, I thought, and stopped pushing him away. I watched his face. And then it was the click, except just for a split second instead of Adam's face belonging to someone I didn't know it was Fred's face I was seeing. And I got really excited.

'You were shouting,' he told me afterwards.

'So were you,' I said. I was worried that his parents had heard us, but when we went downstairs they sounded normal, so I don't think they could have. They wanted us to stay for tea but Adam said he had an essay to do. His parents kissed me goodbye as well as him.

'Don't let him bully you,' Mr Flynn said, which I didn't get. He wanted to drive us back to Adam's but Adam said we'd get the tube. They both stood at the front gate and waved us off down the street.

'How much was the cheque for, then?' I asked him.

'None of your business,' he said.

'What are you going to buy with it?'

'Dunno.'

'You could buy yourself a watch.'

'Ooh, exciting.'

'All right, it was just a suggestion.'

'I've got a watch anyway,' he said. 'I just never wear it, that's all.'

I walked quicker so he had to keep up with me. He tried to hold my hand but I didn't feel like it.

'Why d'you go out with me, Adam?' I asked him.

He looked like I was barmy or I'd just said something in a foreign language. He kept quiet. Then when we got to the tube station he said, 'I told you.'

'What?'

'My fucking parents.'

'What's it got to do with them?' I said.

Adam went over to the ticket machine. He said not to bother, he'd get my ticket as well. I was thinking about Fred, and whether it'd be really stupid to tell Adam about him. When we're both in a better mood, I will, probably. After I've definitely not seen Fred for a while, obviously. Which I won't be. I could ring him to tell him, but it only seems fair to let him know face to face.

Spectre

The voice starts in the dark.

From the elegant club rooms of Mayfair to exotic island night spots. It's a man's voice, like a black cat's fur. James is in a casino, drinking from a wide glass, and then dancing with a lady with shiny hair in a shiny dress, too tight for her to dance back in, so she does tiny, stupid steps. James is wearing his white jacket and a black bow tie. He is looking over the lady's shoulder at a gun which points out from a red velvet curtain.

A strange adventure of intrigue, treachery and love . . . James, in a speedboat, shoots at a man in another speedboat which is trying to catch up with him. At the last minute James swerves away from a small island that has appeared in the middle of the water. The baddie doesn't see this and his boat explodes, filling the picture with orange clouds. Then James is snogging another lady, this time with shiny black hair instead of blonde, then he is shooting out of his car, which almost crashes quite a few times before it goes off a cliff. Fortunately James jumps out of it and roly-polys out of the way before it explodes, filling the picture with orange clouds. The next time he is wearing all black, polo neck and trousers and belt, which looks best because it matches his hair.

The world's greatest gentleman agent with a licence to kill.

'We've seen this one on the telly,' I whisper.

James shushes me. 'It'll be good,' he says. 'I saw this when I was your age.'

'But I've already seen it.'

He shushes me again. He's undercover, strictly. No one else has recognised him except me. Fortunately I am there to act as a decoy. I leave the end of the ice lolly in my mouth until it dissolves, then advance the next bit in. In front of the screen the curtains, which have patterns like the ones you get when you shut your eyes hard and press your hands against your eyeballs, close, wait for a moment, then open.

The lolly suddenly melts into two big lumps and I can only hold one, so the other one has to go in my mouth, which isn't very nice for a couple of seconds before my teeth get used to it. On the screen is the swirling black and white pattern with a circle cut out of it. The circle moves to keep up with James walking in the distance. He stops, wheels round and aims a gun out of nowhere, right at the middle of the circle we can all see him through. There is the loudest bang I've heard in my life. I jump and drop the rest of the lolly, then choke on the piece I have in my mouth. James laughs and thumps me on the back until I stop coughing.

The next bit is practically my favourite, although some of the people watching around us are laughing.

'Students,' James says, so that I know what he thinks of them.

It's like being inside a dream. The title and lots of names swim on to the screen, against a background of ladies who look like shadows, except they're green, then pink, then deepest blue. Sometimes they are small and sometimes so big you only see bits of them, like a hand, or a tipped-up nose and chin having champagne poured over them. They dance to the song that goes with it all, not proper dancing, but a forgetful sort, as though they're doing it on their own with nobody watching. The song makes your neck prickle when it dives into long, loud notes. Then it starts properly and I forget to look at James for ages.

One of the good things, I think, is that you always come in at the end of another film you haven't seen. So either the baddie is killing another agent or hijacking something really important to do with blowing up the world, or James is fighting off baddies to deliver a bit of microfilm. It often involves snow. The baddie kills the other agent, or James wins, and that's that bit over with. Then M asks James into his office to explain why he needs him to do something completely different, which is what we're going to see. But I like the way James is sort of going on whether we see him or not, having other adventures. Which is what he's doing now, I suppose. It's snowing outside as well, or it was when we came in. Not hard, more like scurf on the streets, a bit dirty instead of white. I didn't even know you could see old films at the pictures, but when James saw this was on he got quite excited. It was cheaper as well, he said, than going to a new film. And he'd seen it when he was my age.

'Are you paying attention, 007?'

Q is demonstrating a pen that can be set to emit signals so you can be spotted on radar. It would be helpful in our case, if Pussy Galore had one of these. James told me she's staying with her auntie in Wales but I think this is a cover story, to protect her anonymity. James is at a higher level of security clearance than me. Pussy Galore could in fact be a double agent, and on our side, or a triple agent even, and a baddie. She's never mentioned having an auntie in Wales, but you never know. She doesn't tell me much.

I'm pretty sure that this is James's current mission, to find her. Because no one goes to the seaside in February. Of course we're not in Wales, but that doesn't mean anything. We'll probably go there eventually, because James is used to travelling. He usually has to go to three or four places, not counting getting captured, before he finds the villain's lair. Like now, he's in this lady's room at the hotel, which you know is a big mistake, because either she's going to hit him over the head with something or give him an injection to knock him out when he's not looking, or he'll nod off to sleep and they'll both get clobbered by baddies coming into the room. And whatever happens, when he wakes up he'll be somewhere completely different. Luckily he has all the stuff that Q has given him, so once the baddie has told him how he wants to take over all the water in the world, or all the rockets, or all the diamonds, James can escape.

Our room in the hotel looks nothing like the one up there. For one thing our room is about twice the size of the bed James and the lady are on put together. In our room you can walk from the bed to the dressing table to the door easily without touching the floor. I know because I tried it out when we arrived. This is good practice for if, for example, the baddies flood your room with water then fill it with sharks or piranhas or something. It's harder than it looks because the mattress is fairly lumpy and that puts you off balance, but I got quite quick after a couple of goes. James didn't tell me not to. Even when I did trampolining training on my side of the bed, to improve my skills, he just stayed on his side, smoking. Then I hit my head accidentally on the headboard when I was trying to do a somersault, and he said that was my fault, and I'd better stop now before the landlady kicked us out. My head hurt quite a lot and I had to rub it extremely hard to stop myself from crying, which obviously you have to be trained not to do. James never cries, ever.

Quite soon I think I'm going to have to learn how to smoke as well.

Just as I suspected, the lady has put knock-out drops in James's martini. I'd always take my own if I was on a secret mission, in a flask. When James said we were going to the seaside I was going to get the flask with the tartan sides we always take to the seaside, for the journey, but James wouldn't even let me look for it. He said there wasn't time. Pussy Galore might have taken it to Wales with her anyway, although she didn't take anything else. I looked in her side of the wardrobe before we left and all her clothes were there, including the blue dress James says makes her look fat. I sniffed it and it smelt of her Mum deodorant.

Without the flask I got thirsty on the journey so James bought me a can of Coke when he stopped to get petrol. Unfortunately it was too fizzy and he had to stop the car so that I could be sick by the side of the road. That is the sixth time ever I have been sick, not counting the times when I was a baby I can't remember.

That's another thing that James never does. You could make a list as follows of things James never does.

1. Be sick.
2. Cry.
3. Go to the toilet.
4. Go shopping.
5. Wait for buses.
6. Play football.
7. Watch telly.
8. Visit people, like aunties. In fact, he doesn't have any aunties.

'A pleasure, Commander Bond.'

You can always tell baddies because they're very polite. James is polite as well, but he makes jokes which the baddies don't like. He makes jokes when he shoots people or blows them up too. They deserve it, because they're baddies. I don't always get the jokes, to tell you the truth. When he makes jokes at home Pussy Galore doesn't get them either because she never laughs. The opposite, in fact. Her lips disappear, like the jokes push them inside her mouth.

Anyway, the above list is obviously just in films, because I know James goes to the toilet and watches telly. He doesn't like going shopping, because Pussy Galore complains about it, but he does pay for things. Like last night we were having tea in a caff and James ordered egg and chips for me because we'd had fish and chips three days running and it slipped his mind that I only like egg and chips at home, not when other people make it. The egg was frilly and brown at the edges, so I had to cut that off, and the yolk wasn't runny but set hard like powder, so I couldn't eat that. I was eating though, little bites with just my front two teeth, of the white bits that weren't either frilly and brown or didn't touch the yolk, but James thought I wasn't eating at all and lost his temper and tried to make me eat the wrong bits so I stopped eating and cried and said I wanted to go home. I don't usually cry, but it just came out, like coughing or sneezing. The other people in the caff were looking at us as well but I didn't even care.

James took me outside. It was really dark, and my breath came out the same as James's, although he was smoking. I tried to blow rings with my hot breath but it didn't work. It never does, I don't know why. I'd stopped crying really but sometimes when I breathed in it shivered a bit against the leftover tears in my throat, or maybe just because it was cold. James got hold of my hand, as if I was a little kid, and we walked down the dark street to the pier. The lights were so bright on the amusement arcades they were like a noise in your eyes, pink and white and yellow and blue. I'm not allowed inside arcades, because blokes go in there who do things to you if you're not careful, things with their willies like men in cars with sweets. They don't look bad when you see them from the outside, but they're probably polite like Blofeld.

We walked past a shop without a proper front window or door, more like a shed, open to the street like on a market. It was covered with buckets and spades and fishing nets and cuddly toys and plastic toys on cards, like a flower that had come out before all the other stalls around it, closed and waiting for summer. The man in charge had a radio on next to him to cheer him up.

James stopped and said I could choose a toy, so Pussy Galore's wrong about shopping. At first I thought I'd get a spud gun, but James told me I didn't want it and besides, where would we get the potatoes from, although I suggested a shop. Then I thought of a fishing net, but James said it was too cold to be messing about in the sea. To be honest, a lot of the stuff was for littler kids. I finally chose a blue sort of wallet thing with a notebook in it as well. It has a zip, purple piping and a clear bit at the front with a little mirror in it, and a blue pencil held with a loop of elastic. I thought it would be useful for taking notes and holding equipment, the sort of thing Q might give you, and also you can use the mirror to make signals when you're stranded somewhere. It says 'Made in China' on it, which means it's crap really. James has never bought me anything before, apart from Father Christmas stuff, which Pussy Galore gets anyway. James probably gives her the money and everything, though. He's got better things to do.

James is now strapped to a table, spread out like a starfish. A laser is moving closer and closer, about to cut him in half. He's working his wrist to get it free from the strap so he can undo all the other bits and escape. The laser moves along. His wrist wriggles, his eyebrows lift with effort. The table smokes in a trail behind the moving laser. A final wrench and James's hand is free. Just as the laser begins to burn his trousers, he rolls out of the way. Now he can go and find out what the baddie's up to. I look round at James to share it getting to the good bit and he's gone. He must have got up to go to the toilet. I sit on the edge of my seat and try to concentrate on the film, but it's difficult. A light saying GENTS glows green on one side of the screen, matched by one glowing LADIES on the other. As James snakes round the secret headquarters, karate-chopping a guard so he can steal his uniform, the door to the Gents opens and a shadow man comes out. But as he walks to our row he turns into a real man and he isn't James.

I feel a bit frightened at the top of my stomach, like I've swallowed a hot stone. What if James has gone to the toilet and a SPECTRE agent has got him or he's been taken poorly? I'll have to go into the Gents and if he's not there I'll have to ask someone and I'm not supposed to talk to strangers. I hold my breath by accident, thinking about it. Then fortunately I see not just one policeman but two walking down the Ladies aisle, with their caps on. The usher sweeps her torch along a row in front of the policemen but they don't stop. She does the same thing on the next row, and the next, stirring up grumbling from the people in the audience. It makes sense, policemen seeing the film, because they could pick up quite a few tips, and if anything's happened to James I'll be able to call them without even having to dial 999. There are plenty of seats next to James and me because we're right at the back and off to one side and it's all pretty empty, except for the students.

The door to the Gents opens again and this time I'm almost sure the shadow man is James. Up there, he's running, trying to get into the cockpit of a plane and dancing out of the way of bullets. James walks towards me and the light flicks over him from the torch and I can see it's definitely him. He jumps back from the light as though it's burned him and spins round to see the policemen. Then he runs. He runs up the aisle to where a green sign glows EXIT and he disappears through the soft curtains. I stand up in surprise so my seat snaps upright and I shout, 'James!'

The policemen shove their way across a row, which makes people complain, and they follow James out, swallowed by the curtains. I get up and follow them, to explain they've made a mistake. There are two lots of stairs coming out, which join together at a landing and turn into one big staircase going down to the lobby. The policemen are already on the big staircase and I can't see James at all. He must be out on the street, which isn't surprising because he's a fast runner. I'm not, and also I'm not great at stairs because I have to look where I'm going. The sound from the film is louder out here than inside, but blurred.

'Now Mr Bond, time for you to die.'

The tremendous noise of an explosion chases me as I reach the landing where the staircases join. Below, one of the policemen, the less fat one, is pulling James back into the lobby from outside, holding his coat collar so hard that he's already torn it. James is twisting like a fish on a hook, which is making the tear worse. He's only had that coat since Christmas as well. Pussy Galore will go spare, she says he never looks after things. I close my eyes tight and hope that a button on his coat is a secret ejector button and he'll go crashing up through the roof, but he doesn't. The fatter policeman comes up the stairs to get me before I can run away.

James doesn't talk to me at the police station, and I don't talk to the policemen. It's hot in the room where they make us wait, and someone has spilt something sticky on my plastic chair. The strip light buzzes and flicks like it's just been switched on, but never quite jumps into a proper line of brightness. James has his head in his hands, so I can see his watch. It's almost midnight when a new policeman comes through the door. I think I might have been asleep because I thought I was standing on the beach fishing with a net like the ones they sell at the stalls and catching 50p pieces.

The new policeman doesn't wear a uniform, but a brown suit. He has a beige shirt and beige skin.

'James,' he says.

I think they might know each other. Maybe he works for M. He holds the door open, wide enough for three people to go through. James stands up and goes through the door. The beige policeman smiles at me, more of a twitch than a smile, then closes the door.

This is very good training, this is exactly what they do, they isolate you, it's called, to make you talk. I have decided not to talk at all, like James. Even when the lady policeman comes and gives me a cup of warmish orange juice and asks if I want a bourbon or a custard cream, I don't say anything. She pushes a plate over with both kinds of biscuit on it but I don't take them. She smells of Mum deodorant, although she doesn't look like Pussy Galore at all. The hot stone comes back again, this time into my throat. If it moves up any further it'll come out as crying, so it's a good job I've decided not to say anything. Also, I really want to go to the bog. It's reached the stage where it hurts, but obviously I can't ask. If the lady policeman wasn't there I could sneak out and look round, but she seems to have been sent to guard me. I decide just to have a custard cream, and definitely leave the bourbon. I work my way round the edges, sucking the bare biscuit away up to the filling. Then I prise the top biscuit off, and rake the custard part with my front teeth, the way I'm not allowed to at home.

The lady policeman brings out a pack of cards which she must have had in her pocket. 'How about a game of Snap?' she says, like I'm five years old or something. I don't say anything. James plays cards a lot in the films, but not usually Snap. I don't know what the game is, but he wins money doing it, and everyone is very dressed up. The lady policeman starts to play. It's difficult not to say 'snap' because she's quite slow at spotting the same cards. But since I don't say anything, she wins all the cards, quickly. I let just a bit of pee go into my pants. It makes me feel better but not for very long. I wish I knew karate like James because then I could karate-chop the guard and fight my way out of the police station.

'Don't worry,' the lady policeman says, but she looks at the cards, not me. I remember my blue notebook, I've left it at the pictures. Maybe a bit later I'll be able to mention it to James and we can go over and get it. Not that it's worth much or anything.

Actually, another thing that James really does that's on the list as well as shopping is cry. The night we got to the seaside I woke up and I could hear him a bit. It didn't sound wet like proper crying. It was more like the noise you make when you fall off your bike and the wind's knocked out of you and you're surprised, but he was making that noise over and over again, each time he breathed. I made myself go back to sleep before it sounded like crying, like the way you can when you wake up and people are talking to each other downstairs, even shouting sometimes, and you can make yourself go back to sleep before the words mean anything, even when they're really loud. You just make yourself.

We play another game of Snap with me not playing before the lady policeman gives up. She feels stupid saying 'snap' on her own, I can tell, because she laughs every time she does it. I let a little more pee go, but it's horrible having wet pants and I'm worried about the wet showing on my tracksuit bottoms. Pathetic. I think of James, probably strapped to a table somewhere, with a laser biting towards him. Maybe Pussy Galore will rescue him, and me. If she's not a double agent. Or rather, she is, which means she's on our side. Even though she kisses James and they're in bed and everything she's really supposed to be a baddie.

The door opens and I think everything's going to be all

right now, but it's not anyone I know, it's a lady with long pale hair and long, droopy clothes. She smiles at me properly.

'I bet you're really tired, lovey,' she says. 'Come on.'

She holds out her hand, wanting me to hold it, as if we'd known each other for ages. She's got lots of bracelets on her arm.

'I'm Anne,' she says. 'Do you want to go to the toilet before we go?' I nod. Nodding's not the same as talking. The lady policeman comes with us to show us where the toilet is. Anne waits for me when I go in. I'm pretty sure she's on our side.

'OK?' she says, and opens the door for me. She doesn't try to hold my hand. She touches my shoulder to help me out of the door, although I'm perfectly capable. I bet James has escaped already. He'll probably scale the walls of where they're taking me, or maybe Anne has already got him at her house and is acting under his instructions.

'Do you know what SPECTRE stands for?' I ask Anne, before I remember about not speaking.

'No,' she says. 'What?'

She doesn't look like she's lying, so that means she can't be working for them, because they'd have told her what it means. I don't say anything else. In my head I tell her, though. It stands for Special Executive for Crime, Terror, Revenge and Extortion. James told me that, when I asked. I'm not exactly sure what extortion is, to tell you the truth, but James will tell me when I see him again.

The Lessons of History

This you should know: my entire family is mad. I know, I know, everyone's family is, except for the ones, maddest of all, who claim they aren't. But we're the genuine article. My mother finally managed to commit suicide last year, after years of attempting it, on and off, and my father has barely made sense since the mid-1980s, although he continues to write irate daily letters to the broadsheets. My little brother has just dropped out of university because he's too addled by recreational drugs to continue and I rely on Prozac and various therapists to keep me functioning. Only my sister is normal.

Ergo, she's the maddest of the lot of us.

For a start, she claims our mother died of natural causes. My sister's name is Siena, by the way, but she goes by Susanna, a decision she took unilaterally at eleven.

'You just like the idea of a tragic death,' she accuses me, when I visit her some time after Mum's funeral. I always have to brace myself before I go into her house. It abounds in horrific outbreaks of cartoon post-modernism, gleaned from watching too many DIY makeover programmes.

'You think it's romantic or something.'

'Bollocks,' I quip.

On the ivory rag-rolled wall above the breakfast bar where we sit, Siena, or one of the decorators she employs, has painted *Breakfast* . . . in gigantic black italics. This consigns us to a category error, since we're both eating vegetable lasagne, it being dinnertime. I wonder if Siena and her husband Nick (tall, fund manager, no eyelashes) have *Fucking* . . . written above their grotesquely draped reproduction sleigh bed.

'D'you know that Fred West made a sign to go over his and Rosemary's bed in Cromwell Street, like the one outside his house,' I tell her, 'except it said "cunt"?'

Siena ignores me. Throughout the evening, she retreats from such diversions and doggedly pursues the subject of Mum, reminding me of childhood ordeals in Hampton Court maze, when Siena would resolutely forge an exit while I sobbed statically over being lost. Her line is that Mum was confused and impractical at the best of times (true), and there was nothing more understandable than her taking a few Valium too many and then foolishly climbing into a hot bath. Since the coroner reached the same conclusion, Siena feels that she can't be gainsaid.

(I was very disappointed in the coroner, if truth be known. I was expecting a whip-smart, mean-eyed character from an American film, not a doughy bloke in a bad suit. When we met him he kept getting Mum's name wrong.)

'Mum was depressed,' I insist.

'Who isn't?' says Siena, and smartly loads the dishwasher, which is pointlessly concealed by a sort of curtain made of corded tassels. 'If everyone who was a bit depressed killed themselves . . .'

'Not a bit depressed,' I exclaim. 'Depressed, capital D. Big time.'

Siena pulls a couple of the tassels free from the dishwasher door. They look mangy, like they've been through the wash a time or two.

'I think you like the idea of Mum committing suicide because it makes you feel better about yourself,' she says, all composure.

Once I'm at home, in bed, I add a line to this interchange:

'How Californian of you,' I retort.

Most of the summer goes by. August, the therapists' period of exodus, is always a difficult month for me. I can't afford a holiday to take my mind off it of course, because my disposable income goes on therapy. And all my friends are away, even the ones I don't particularly like. Dad rings up once, excited, to tell me to buy the *Daily Telegraph*. He's actually got a letter in, about the England cricket team. This is a first for him, although he's succeeded with the *Times* once or twice over the years. Before he hangs up he informs me that my brother has gone to Devon for a festival, and that Siena and Nick are due to go to France for a couple of weeks with their kids. Naturally Mum isn't mentioned.

He's done a kind of Stalinist rewrite on her and seems to have lived a bachelor life since time immemorial. Which is effectively true, come to think of it.

A few days later the phone rings so early that when my gummed eyes open, the world isn't yet in colour, or fully resolved, but offers uncertain edges in a variety of wan greys.

'Have you heard?' It's Siena. Her voice, freighted with panic, strikes a chord at the pit of my stomach.

'What?'

'She's been in an accident. They said it was serious—'

'Is Dad all right?'

'Dad?'

'What's wrong?'

I'm still more asleep than awake. I think she's talking about Mum. Mum's alive and she's been in an accident.

'Princess Diana. I've been listening to the radio for hours and Nick is away—'

Siena's wired, gabbling, wanting to talk. To talk to me, which clinches the oddity of her condition. Although a salvaging sense of the normal has perhaps alerted her to the unsuitability of ringing up any actual friends in the middle of the night, she obviously thinks unstable siblings are fair game.

'Dodi was killed instantly but they're operating on her now. It's the World Service . . .'

Some of her excitement leaps across to me. I can see why she had to talk to someone.

'Really?'

Her voice accelerates.

'Their car crashed while they were being chased by reporters. That's what they're saying, anyway . . .'

Although we don't admit what's keeping us talking, there's an appalling pleasure in the bizarre novelty of it, its unreal reality. After some minutes of agitated speculation, Siena hangs up to catch the next news bulletin, and I cruise my crappy radio for the World Service. When we hear the report of Diana's death, we speak again, to confirm it for each other.

Through the next day and the next week I keep the TV on with the sound turned down, as if something else is going to happen, as if something extra can occur to surpass this perfect catastrophe. Habituated to air disasters and serial killers, I crave a multiplicity of deaths to make this one truly satisfactory. The montages of Diana's life screened constantly during this time help in this respect. There's always a *frisson* when the clips come to an end, like the small visceral jarring of a continuity error. Each of these, a tiny renewed surprise at finality, adds to the value of that single death.

It's the day before the funeral when I pick out Siena on the TV, packed in the crowd outside Kensington Palace. She's only on the screen for half a second as the camera pans across the myriad grieving faces, but I'm sure it's her, the heavy swing of her hair as she turns her head. I didn't spend my adolescence envying every strand of her hair not to recognise it when it's in front of me. I phone her later to get the complete bread and circuses low-down, but Nick answers instead. He says that she's having an early night, but confirms that it was indeed Siena (Susanna, as he always calls her) outside the palace.

'She's taken it pretty hard,' he then tells me, all sub-dued modulation. I don't know what to say to this. As far as I am aware Siena has the same profound detachment con-cerning the Royal Family as most people, and I'd presumed that she'd fetched up in Kensington out of a healthy desire to ogle. But Nick says that Siena's taken time off work, she's been brought so low by the princess's death. That's what he calls it, 'the princess's death'. His tone is empty of irony, although he's highly capable of it. I'm usually sur-prised by how human a being Nick is when I actually talk to him, lack of eyelashes notwithstanding, but on this occasion he more than lives down to the sister's-banker-husband stereotype.

Still, I feel a little gleeful. *She's lost it*, I think. And it seems over the next weeks that she might have, in a minor way. She and Nick cancel their holiday, for a start, because Siena isn't feeling up to it. When she tells me this on the phone, with a new, invalid quaver to her voice, I contrive an invitation for dinner. I want to plumb and savour this mad-ness at first hand, if it really exists.

I don't have long to wait. Nick is at home, although the kids are in bed, and the three of us eat lamb couscous under the *Breakfast* . . . sign. Siena takes up the subject of Diana's death without incitement, as though continuing a pre-exist-ing conversation. Nick shows neither alarm nor disapproval, and I go with the flow, remarking that it's a shame Diana died just when she'd got on top of her personal style.

'You can see it in the clips,' I say, convincing myself as I talk. 'The Sloane frilly collar thing, then the prematurely middle-aged sort of county frump, then the *Dynasty* thing,

and the Essex gym queen or whatever, and just at the end
she looked quite chic. You know, that simple white bathing
suit—'

'Jesus *Christ*!' exclaims Siena, slamming down her fork.
Her emphasis scares me mute. 'Don't you think of *anything*
except the way things look?' She bows her head, bracing
herself to convey something of importance. 'She was a –
real – person!'

I start to deny this, but Siena has burst into tears. Not
tears of offence, but of pain: she convulses, her nose runs,
she wails as wholeheartedly as a little girl maliciously
tripped in the playground. I have no memory of her crying
in the last ten years, not even when Mum was signed off. It
takes some time for her to subside, with Nick comforting
her. I apologise, and then sit in silence as she condemns (at
some length) the House of Windsor for their fatal lack of
feeling. Nick sheepishly sees me off at the door, before pudding can be broached. I've spent better evenings.

Truth to tell, seeing Siena so affected has made me feel
slightly panicky. It's one thing to gloat at the demise of a
control freak, quite another to witness her total disintegration. And rampant monarchism with a necrophiliac slant
runs a close second to the fervent embrace of Jesus Christ
the Saviour of Mankind as Least Wanted New Trait in a
Close Relative. Mercifully, my therapist is due back shortly
from holiday, and in the meantime I steer clear of family
invitations, sparse as they tend to be.

Given this policy, there's no way I would have heard
about Siena's arrest if Nick hadn't been in Germany on one
of his business trips. In his absence, Siena phones me from

the police station, leaving an unconvincingly sedate message on my answerphone, setting out the fact of her arrest and the police station where she's being held. There's a subsequent, even more composed message, apologising for her previous message, and reassuring me that she's been the victim of a misunderstanding and has consulted a lawyer.

'No need to worry Dad,' she concludes, with forced brightness. (As though I would. As though even this would permeate his self-obsession, unless he sensed new material for a letter condemning high-handed behaviour by the Met.) Despite Siena's assurances I ring the police station, making contact with a world which seems seriously awry. I've seen Siena pick up other people's litter in the street, she pays her tax bills early, as far as I know she's never even had a parking ticket: I simply can't imagine the nature of any crime she might be provoked to commit. After some time on hold I get through, and with a little cajoling they tell me what it is she's done.

She was caught nicking some flowers from the rotting, mountainous tribute to Diana outside Kensington Palace.

'What kind of flowers?' I ask the desk sergeant. Although he's irritated by the question, he goes and finds the form where her felony is specified.

'Carnations,' he announces.

My first thought is that she's been framed. Siena wouldn't give house room to any flower so tainted by its associations with petrol stations. She goes in for exorbitantly priced exotics that look like triffids. But when I find it in my heart to get round to the police station, because they won't let me speak to her on the phone and they're holding her until she appears in the magistrates' court the next morning, she admits the theft.

'Why?' I ask her, bewildered. Siena's eyes are rubbed clean of mascara but she seems otherwise composed. Her shrug is disturbingly familiar, from the realm of her usual behaviour. There's a nasty faecal undertow corrupting the disinfectant tang of the custody cell air. I imagine drunk and disorderlies, GBH and affrays. People for whom shitting themselves is the least of their worries.

'There were so many flowers I didn't think it would make a difference,' she says. Reasonable.

'Yes, but why did you want them in the first place?' I persist. To this, she just shrugs again, and sighs blankly.

'Anyway,' she says, and with one hand twitches her jacket in to her waist, where it fastens. This is a gesture so familiar to me from our mother that seeing it appropriated by my sister is shocking, like witnessing a split second of ghostly possession. Mum used it to signify the end of a difficult conversation, as far as she was concerned. The movement is no less effective as a hand-me-down. The simple doing up of Siena's button unbuttons in me all the rage I'm stuffed with.

'I don't know what's wrong with you!' I shriek. 'You didn't know the woman! For God's sake – what did she ever do for you? Some Sloaney airhead! You didn't even care about her when she was alive!'

Siena matches me for pitch and volume, hissing saliva as she shouts.

'I've always taken an interest. And you forget what she did—'

'I don't care if she was nice to people with AIDS! You make me sick!'

And so on. When I hear myself yelling that she committed suicide it becomes apparent that I'm no longer certain what's upsetting me. Siena gets hold of me and we clutch each other, more hostile than comforting, almost grappling. The wool blend of her jacket is severe against my cheek. She's crying too, I realise, a mirror of my own distress. We have never cried in unison before, not that I can remember. The phrase 'it's come to this' suggests itself to me, gratuitously adorning the moment like the script on Siena's kitchen wall.

We pull apart.

'I suppose it'll all sort of just be – over – in a few weeks. I wanted . . .' her voice has collapsed, deflated of its usual rubbery confidence. 'Oh I don't know.'

Her appearance in the magistrates' court is a non-event. Siena/Susanna is not, as recent miscreants have been, a teddy-purloining foreigner out for dubious personal gain, but a solid citizen of the Home Counties, a wife, mother and, most importantly, a genuinely stricken mourner. They let her off with a token fine and a cluster of media interest outside the court. This she fobs off, but still makes the early evening news. Dad chances to see this, but any concern over the event is superseded by his excitement at seeing a family member on TV. I think he considers it a generational development of his own ambition to appear in print. Barking, you see.

Everyone steers clear of the Subject. Even my sister seems to mention it less as the months pass. Nick airs no view on the matter, and continues to provide quiet support while doing any despairing of his wife's lapse from rectitude behind the scenes. And on my part these shenanigans, the mere existence of shenanigans attaching themselves so uncharacteristically to my sister, have forced a curious fondness into bloom. We make an effort, and do proper things together, things that people who actually like each other would do, instead of the grudging reciprocity of our previous social arrangements. One such, towards Christmas, is a shopping trip to Knightsbridge. This is Siena's suggestion. I'm feeling a touch agoraphobic but quell it for her sake.

We do Harrods last. Harrods always reminds me of an anxiety dream, and sure enough we get lost while we're looking for the stationery department, and have to stumble through shelves and barrows piled with merchandise stamped with 'Harrods' before we can find a relevant turning. I am about to strike out in the right direction when Siena touches my arm, diverting me.

'Look!'

There's a free-standing sign, of the kind used by not very nice restaurants to ask you to wait to be seated, except this one is gold. It reads THE DIANA AND DODI MEMORIAL. Siena is already on her way. I follow her out of the door.

At the foot of the escalator is what looks to be a bower, or shrine. As we get closer I see that it's actually a fountain. Its centrepiece is a gilded, sinuously art nouveau entwining of lily-like flutes and tendrils which form twin picture frames. These enclose vivid, badly reproduced shots of the dead lovers, sycophantically lit. Diana's picture is one of the glamorous ones with a fringe she had taken for that book. Dodi's looks like it might have been extracted and blown up from a group shot – the focus is not absolute enough for a portrait. As photographs, the pair don't match.

I hover for an attenuated minute, for my sister's sake. We are not alone, although Siena is the only visitor to bow her head. There are many coins in the shallow scallops of the fountain. A sign to the right explains that these are destined for charity, and a table to the left contains a heap of flowers left by those paying their respects. I think of our mother. There has been talk of planting a rose bush in her and Dad's garden. Not that she liked roses particularly. There wasn't much that she particularly liked, when I think of it.

Siena speaks in a church hush. 'You know that Al Fayed is close to exposing the agents behind it,' she murmurs.

It takes me a second to work out the meaning of this.

'It was an accident,' I protest, at a normal level.

She smirks. 'Oh come on. D'you really think the Royal Family would have allowed her to marry a Muslim?'

Her hand reaches beneath the encumbrance of her winter coat for the imaginary button at her waist. I look away. In the silence of an argument we'll never have, we retrace our steps and, after a moment to get our bearings, press on to the stationery department.

Driving from Memory

Waking into this light dilutes nostalgia's essence. Here I am, in the place where I can't go back. This resinous breath I draw in, the give of the mattress against my spine, the trails of light on the ceiling careening against each other in diamond points as they reflect the lake water. Only the undertow of mould is different. And my brother, in the bed next to mine.

But he isn't there. The covers are empty, and it's the noise of him moving around that has woken me. The screen door whines and I hear his steps tamping down the undergrowth outside. Maybe he plans to start a fire. The tip of my nose has been chilled by the air. As he promised last night, summer is over.

I need to pee quite badly. The toilet in the cottage is

unconnected, and I know I'll have to use the privy outside.
I pull clothes over the T-shirt and socks I've been wearing all
night, warmed by my body. As the pattern on the ceiling
promised, it's a bright day, the sunny lake visible even
through the thick trees that have thickened around the cottage since I was last here. It reminds me of Sleeping Beauty,
except her castle was enclosed by brambles, as I remember,
and it's mostly pines that have edged in on my father's hand-
iwork.

'Sleep OK?' asks Michael. He's standing looking at the
little log shelter, still half full of neatly stacked logs that
have rotted into uselessness.

'Dead to the world,' I say. 'I'm going to brave the kazi.
You're all right, you can pee standing up.'

He smiles.

'D'you think it's fit to use?' I ask him.

I haven't peed, I realise, since we stopped off at the
chicken restaurant last night.

'Don't know. Want me to check?'

'It's all right. I'll scream if I need any help.'

'OK. You know what poison ivy looks like. If there's
nothing else to wipe yourself on.'

I go back into the cottage and get some tissues from my
bag. I think that's Michael's way of joking. I can't do deadpan; I signal with my face and use verbal parentheses in case
any irony is held against me. But then we come from a different culture. He watches me go up the gravel track.

'You want coffee?' he asks.

'Please,' I shout.

The door of the privy is swollen open and I have to kick

away a heap of leaf litter to get through. It is as remembered and feared. The tiny window webbed over, but with no spider resident, insect scuttlings across the wooden seat, a sour, semi-chemical stench. I don't look in the hole when I lift the cover aside, but my heart jolts when there is a scuffling below as a reaction to the influx of light. After freezing for a couple of seconds to reassure myself that there are no further sounds I pee, balancing on my cold hands to keep a distance from the hole.

'Mission accomplished,' I say to Michael, who is boiling water on the stove. 'Hey, you got the gas going.'

'It's no problem,' he says. 'But the water's a real pain, you know?'

'You've tried?'

'I've tried the pump, but there's nothing happening. I mean, it seems OK – I think the line is shot. Could've rotted, or a porcupine's gnawed through or something. We'd have to check it all the way to the lake.'

'Oh well, let's not bother,' I say. 'It's not worth it for a couple of days.'

'That's what I figured,' he says. 'We'll have to get someone out to fix it if we decide to sell. Even if we don't, I guess.'

My brother sells life insurance. There is no reason for him to be an expert on water pumps or gas or what he calls hydro. But I have been relying on him to get things working. I think it is because he looks like my father. Although as he makes the coffee I see the resemblance has more to do with his height and the plaid wool shirt he is wearing than any real physical similarity. Apart from the height, I take after our father more. I am fair, like him, and soft-featured. My brother has thinning black hair and what some people call a Roman nose. Perhaps around the eyes we look alike.

We take our coffee out on to the sun deck and sit on the steps to drink it. It is no colder than inside the cottage, and smells better.

'Are you forty-five now, Michael?' I ask.

'Forty-four next month,' he says.

'You realise that you're nearly the age Dad was when I last saw him?'

'Is that right?'

'He must have been forty-eight.'

Michael thinks about this. 'I guess so. Seventy's not so old to die these days.'

We drink our coffee, which is bitterly good.

'I forgot it was so long,' says Michael. 'Wait a second.'

He goes out to the car and comes back with some photos. They are of Dad, some on his own and some with Michael and his wife Sarah and their two boys.

'Christ,' I say. 'He looks so old.'

'Well, he wasn't doing too good for the last few years.'

In one of the photos, Dad sits on a lawn chair on a patio, his legs stretched in front of him. He is wearing shorts, and on the left leg the white sock and brown desert boot I remember him favouring. The other leg finishes above the ankle in a wadded bundle of fabric. My father looks sorry for himself and his missing foot, although he may just be squinting against the sun. Beneath the peak of his baseball cap, also a familiar style, one of his eye sockets is apparently shrivelled.

'I didn't know about his eye,' I say.

'That was the diabetes as well. Couldn't see a thing. He kept on driving, you know, when he should have handed in his licence. Sarah wouldn't get in the car with him, or let him take the kids anywhere.'

'I don't blame her.'

'Yeah. He told me once that he was driving from memory. Pretty scary. But even when he crashed it he just blamed the other drivers.'

'That sounds like him.'

Michael takes the photos from where I've laid them on the step and puts them back in their paper wallet.

'I guess I forget what you know about him. You were so young when you left.'

'Eleven isn't really tiny. And Mum kept it going too, with her stories.'

A small silence hangs between us. Our father divorced Michael's mother shortly after meeting my mother.

'I'd forgotten how the trees sound like the sea,' I say for something to say. 'The leaves, I mean.'

'They're overrunning the place. I did some cutting back when we were here three years ago but they've taken over again. The old man even helped. Sarah thought he was going to take his own foot off with the saw – it was before the operation.'

Of course Michael and his family visited the cottage fairly regularly until our father got really ill. I have been seeing it neglected for the whole twenty years since my last visit, but that is not the way things are.

We are silent again, then by some trick of synchronicity

stir and pick up our cups simultaneously. We smile shyly at each other, mutual foreigners who use broad gestures of goodwill to stand in for a more nuanced understanding. We go inside.

Neither of us has had a really good look round the cottage since our arrival. Very little has altered against the inventory I hold in my memory. There are shelves packed with *National Geographic* and *Reader's Digest* magazines dating back to the early 1960s, when the cottage was built. There are abstract parts of farm implements on the walls, salvaged by my father from the undergrowth on country walks, de-rusted and painted black. Also on the walls are several paint-by-numbers pictures, sad-eyed kittens and sun-dappled deer rendered in discrete globs of acrylic shaded like khaki ice-cream. These were the legacy of his first heart attack, shortly after the divorce from Michael's mother. During his stay in hospital he produced stacks of these pictures. Some used to hang in the den at home, until my mother gave them to a charity shop while she was decorating. They had one of their rows about that.

Seeing what the cottage contains I realise his mania for making things. Stacked in a corner is a clutch of walking sticks which enchanted me as a child. They were made from the stems of saplings choked by some parasitic vine curling up their trunks. My father removed the vine and varnished the remaining spiralled and indented wood, topping each bizarre bole with a spherical knob and tailing it with a rubber tip. I used to think the resulting canes could only have supported someone of equally eccentric gait and appearance, a lame goblin or halting wizard.

'Jesus, there's some crap here, isn't there?' Michael picks up one of the sticks and I like him a little less. 'I always thought these were useless, you know? But the old man insisted on using one of the goddamn things when he got out of the hospital. Looked like nothing on earth, I'm telling you. He needed the support even when he got the, uh, false leg?'

'The prosthesis.'

'That's it. Look here.' Michael indicates a trail of small black pellets bisecting one of the faded rag rugs. 'We got a mouse problem. You squeamish?'

'Not about mice. Spiders yes.'

'We're going to have to put traps down, clean the place out. You worried about putting traps down?'

'I told you, mice don't bother me.'

'No, I mean, are you worried about them being killed?'

'Michael, I'm not even a vegetarian.'

'No. You just look like one, I guess.' Deadpan again.

We work for a couple of hours, discovering the worst. Every surface in the cottage is covered with greasy dust that has grown into curls in corners. I also come across some insect debris, but I leave it to Michael to explore this more fully. Mice have nested among the blankets in some of the drawers, and there are droppings everywhere, but only once do I disturb a visible mouse, which disappears immediately into some crevice in the wall.

We make piles of things to be disposed of and things to be cleaned. There is also a pile of things to be discussed and possibly allocated, which includes obviously useless but undamaged knick-knacks such as a wooden sign reading

'Old bankers never die, they just lose interest'. On this, my father has scrawled 'oh yeah?' in ballpoint. I haven't seen his handwriting in years, but I know it. He wrote to me when my mother died. Michael and I are very scrupulous about consulting each other before putting anything on the rubbish pile, even though it's mostly decayed towels or twenty-year-old newsprint. By the time we've finished the two bedrooms, the undecided pile is the largest by far.

'Do you want to stop for a while?' asks Michael.

'I can carry on, I mean I'm not tired or anything,' I say, although I'm feeling both tired and hungry.

'Maybe it would be a good idea to go get some stuff from the Falls. I could do with a beer too.'

'OK.'

Michael drives us into town in his big car, with me stopping to open gates on the way. These cut off the track from any wandering cattle. At least that's what I was told as a child. I can't remember seeing any cows, ever. The goldenrod has started to die off, but it still reaches almost to my chest when my body scythes through it to get to the last gate.

The town has changed. Its population has aged, with most of the younger people moving out to places that offer them something more than the occasional shindig at the Legion or the church's strawberry social. Despite this, there is a new pizza parlour and a skating rink. The rink strikes me as a bizarre form of entertainment for a place which is often cut off by snow in the winter, with its surrounding lakes iced over well into April. I say this to Michael.

'Yeah, I guess they didn't work out how many people come here once the season is over,' he says, missing my irony about the ice. I feel slightly homesick.

'I never missed the winters when we left Canada,' I say to Michael.

'They can get you down,' he agrees, parking the car. 'You ski?'

'Do I look like a skier?' I try a little deadpan myself.

'No.' He's better at it.

We go into the general store, which smells the same but looks entirely different. Michael greets the large-bellied man behind the counter with a kind of drawling flirtatious-ness that reminds me of Dad. They each appraise how the other has aged and joke about it a little and establish the health of their families. The man, introduced as Dave, knew my father and expresses regret at hearing of his death. Michael then explains who I am.

'You used to come up here?' Dave asks incredulously. I say that I did, every summer until I was eleven.

Dave shakes his head. 'I'd never have said he had a daugh-ter. Must have forgot if ever I knew. You remember me?'

'I'm afraid not,' I tell him. We swap smiles of vacant friendliness.

'I was skinnier then,' he persists, 'maybe had long hair too.'

'I remember the store.' It's the best I can do. I turn to Michael. 'You used to bring me in here and buy me a pop-sicle.'

We all smile at each other as I pay for several mousetraps. When we leave the store, Michael says that he should find a phone and call Sarah. He asks if I want to eat first. I say no, it's fine if he wants to make a call. I should make one myself.

'Maybe we should eat first, then you can make your call,' he suggests. I sense that he would definitely prefer to do one thing or the other, but I don't know him well enough to guess which. I can't get over the feeling that he is my host, and therefore deferring to me.

'I honestly don't mind,' I say.

'Let's go eat then.'

In the restaurant, he has a hamburger and I order something called a western sandwich because I can't remember having had one before. Michael's description of it is far more appetising than what actually arrives, although he tells me that I haven't been served a good example. Michael finishes his first beer before the food arrives, and orders a second.

'It's thirsty work back there,' he observes. I agree, and another of our silences descends, alleviated by the waitress bringing the plates of food and some minutes of eating. Michael drains his second beer and asks for another.

'Isn't it good?'

He is looking at what I've left on my plate. I tell him that I always leave my crusts.

'You happy?' he asks. His tone never seems to waver from the neutral, or so it sounds to me, so it is impossible to tell whether his question is general or specific.

'Now? I'm tired. I think the jet lag's catching up with me. And maybe it's the air up here. Didn't Dad use to say that the air knocked you out the first couple of days?'

Michael sucks on the mouth of the beer bottle. 'That's what he used to say.'

I dismiss the echo of mockery I hear in this as paranoia. The next beer he has I can't resist counting as his fourth. I decline uneasily when he asks me to join him. But the squat beer bottles are small, the day has turned warm and he is right to claim that what we've been doing has made us thirsty. I crunch the ice cubes in my complimentary glass of water. They taste strongly of chlorine.

'I don't have his problem,' says Michael, cupping the bottle in his hand.

'Sorry?'

He tilts the bottle towards me. 'With this.'

'Oh – no . . .' I'm too embarrassed even to deny what I was thinking. He laughs.

'It's not been for lack of trying, when I was a young guy, you know. But I've got a weak head, weak stomach too. Just can't put them away like he did. This is about my limit.'

I smile and hold the smile. The muscles on each side of my mouth feel the strain of all the smiling I've been doing since I arrived. I remember the kazi and get up to use the toilet before we go. Michael refuses to let me pay the bill. The check, he calls it.

We go to the post office to make our phone calls. There is a bank of credit card phones in the lobby. I calculate the time in England: nearly eight-thirty in the evening. The phone is answered on the third ring.

'It's me,' I say. There is a tiny delay before Mike, my own Michael, responds. His warmth does not entirely compensate for the isolation I feel in that second when I could be anyone.

'What's it like?' he wants to know. 'Describe what you see.'

I tell him that there are lots of maple trees outside beginning to turn gold, and bright sunshine, and next to me my half-brother is making a phone call to his wife in Toronto.

'No Mounties then.'

'No Mounties, no.'

'What's he like?'

'Fine, difficult to know, really. I mean we don't know each other. But fine.'

'And the funeral was OK?'

'Yeah.'

'I really miss you. I've been going around missing you since Thursday.'

'Only since Thursday?'

'Well I've been busy. It didn't really hit me till then.' He pauses, and in the time lag on the transatlantic line his 'Do you miss me?' collides with my 'I miss you'. He tells me that he's reading the Sunday papers, and I can't believe that it's a Sunday here as well. We say goodbye mournfully.

Michael is waiting for me by the door.

'Everything OK?' he asks.

'Yeah. Raining over there as usual. You?'

'Oh Kieran's got a fever. Nothing serious – but you know the way it is with kids – Sarah says if Kieran has it that means Drew's going to get it by tomorrow. She thinks they should stay home.'

'Really?'

'Well, maybe it's the best idea. We can get cleared up here and head back tomorrow night.'

Back at the car, I think about the beers Michael has had at lunch and offer to drive. He declines automatically, as if it were just a polite gesture. I don't press it any more, feeling the guilty comparison with my father. The seat belt on my side is broken. I am nervously aware of this as we pull out on to the highway for the short stretch before turning off on to the unpaved track to the cottage. Hoping that Michael will not notice, I hold the seat belt against my side, as though I would be able to pull it across my body at the moment of impact.

'You going to have kids?' he asks.

'Maybe,' I say.

'Don't,' he says. I know he dotes on Kieran and Drew by the way he puts them down. I thinks he is about to miss the steep turning on to the track, but he spins the wheel abruptly and the car climbs on to it with an unwieldy surge of speed. I reflexively pull out a little more of the seat-belt strap.

'You think you're going to be such hot shit as a parent and I tell you, it's harder than it looks.'

'You seem to be doing OK.'

'So far. You never know what's going to happen when they're teenagers.'

We don't speak again until we're at the cottage. Coming back to it, it already looks more inhabited and tended, although we've done nothing to the outside. Michael says that he'd better check out the tiles on the roof. Some have lifted and need replacing. I offer to help, but he says he's going to wait a couple of hours until it's a little cooler. Even under the screen of trees it's hot, and I have to slap mosquitoes away. I can smell the sweat on myself.

'I think I'd better go down to the lake,' I say. 'I'm beginning to feel a little ripe.'

I don't have anything to swim in, apart from my underwear. Michael says there might be a bathing suit in one of the bedroom drawers. He finds an old pair of his own trunks for himself, but there is nothing suitable for me. After some more rummaging I find a woman's swimming costume pushed to the back of a shelf. It is old fashioned, made of thick polyester printed with psychedelic blue flowers. Although I don't recognise it, it is a style I associate with my mother. There are stiff cups sewn into the bodice, intended to provide uplift for a cleavage far more substantial than mine. I rip out the padded cones and put the suit on, covering it with a T-shirt.

Michael has his plaid shirt on over his costume, which he admits to finding slightly tight. We walk down to the lake. The water is torpid and clear.

'They reckon there's a problem with acid rain,' says Michael. 'That's why there isn't as much weed as there used to be.'

The slatted sections of the dock are stacked by the shore, waiting to be assembled. My father built them too.

'There was the most enormous bullfrog one year, sitting on the steps of the dock. Huge,' I say. Michael doesn't remember. He skims the water with his bare foot.

'Sun's warmed it up,' he says, and walks in. He plunges his body in quickly, whooping with shock at the immersion. 'It's cold underneath!' he shouts, swimming out strongly. Then he stands with the water at his chest and urges me to come in. I intend to edge in more cautiously, but the mud of the lake bottom oozing between my toes feels so unpleasant that I start to swim immediately. It is shallow this near the shore and my thighs and belly scrape the bottom. I kick out into the deeper water.

Michael has been soaping himself. When I reach him his torso and hair are white with lather, and the bar of soap is bobbing in the water next to him. There is only one kind of soap that floats, and this is the kind my father always insisted we buy. I scoop it from the water and smell it. Michael rubs each underarm vigorously in turn.

'This can't be very ecologically sound,' I say.

'The water's fucked anyway. I don't think a little soap's going to make any difference, if you'll excuse my French.'

After so much formality, there is relief in hearing Michael swear. He gulps a breath in, holds it, and slides beneath the water. Then he breaks the surface, blowing, the suds dispersed around him in a widening ring. He has a good body, covered with black hair on the chest and more sparsely on the shoulders, sleeked with the wet. I still have my T-shirt on and now feel self-conscious about taking it off, although it feels heavy and clammy against my skin and I want to be able to wash properly.

'You got a tattoo you don't want me to see or something?' says Michael.

'It's my deeply unfashionable swimsuit I'm ashamed of.'

Michael scuds around in the water. I take the T-shirt off and lather myself quickly, then float on my back to rinse the soap from my hair. Suddenly, Michael breaks into a splashing crawl that beats waves against my body. I right myself. He is making for a rock that sticks out of the horizon. I enter the race, gain on him and pass, arms and legs flailing. My knee grazes the rock as I pull myself on to it. Michael laughs.

'No fair. You didn't say go.' He squirms on to the wet rock, more out of breath than me. The sun is low and soft across the lake. Michael pats the rock.

'Good old Danny Price, eh?'

'You remember?'

I had named the rock after a boy at school I pretended to hate but secretly adored. Michael points to a companion outcrop a couple of yards away.

'Sylvia Pickering. The old man always called them that. Drew and Kieran used to have races to Sylvia Pickering and Danny Price when we came up here a lot.'

'God, Sylvia Pickering's probably got twelve children or won the Nobel Prize or something.'

'What about Danny Price here?'

'In prison probably. Or married to Sylvia Pickering with twelve children.' The sun is behind Michael so that when I squint at him his face is a radiant blur. 'So he remembered that?'

'Oh yeah. He had a lot of things he talked about that you'd said when you were a little kid.'

I want to know what exactly, but I can't ask. I rub my grazed knee.

'What's that on your leg?' Michael asks. I know he doesn't mean the graze.

'I used to cut myself, when I was a teenager. Not badly, just to draw blood.'

'Jesus.'

'It wasn't serious. I used to cut where it didn't show.'

Michael is shaking his head.

'Things are better now,' I say. 'It was a phase.' My flesh is goose-bumping.

'Yeah, they get better, eh?'

I want to touch his large body, but I slither back into the water and swim to the shore. When I reach it he is still perched on Danny Price. He waves to me, stands, then does a cannonball jump with his arms tucked around his legs. For several seconds after the churning impact he is not there at all, and when he reappears it's much closer than I predicted.

Virago now offers an exciting range of quality titles by both established and new authors. All of the books in this series are available from:

Little, Brown and Company (UK),
P.O. Box 11,
Falmouth,
Cornwall TR10 9EN.

Alternatively you may fax your order to the above address. Fax No. 01326 317444.

Payments can be made as follows: cheque, postal order (payable to Little, Brown and Company) or by credit cards, Visa/Access. Do not send cash or currency. UK customers and B.F.P.O.: please send a cheque or postal order (no currency) and allow £1.00 for postage and packing for the first book, plus 50p for the second book, plus 30p for each additional book up to a maximum charge of £3.00 (7 books plus).

Overseas customers including Ireland please allow £2.00 for postage and packing for the first book, plus £1.00 for the second book, plus 50p for each additional book.

NAME (Block Letters) ....

....

ADDRESS ....

....

....

☐ I enclose my remittance for ....

Number ☐☐☐☐☐☐☐☐☐☐☐☐☐☐☐☐☐☐

Card Expiry Date ☐☐☐☐